SWAGGER AND SASS

Lost Kings MC #14.5

AUTUMN JONES LAKE

A LOST KINGS MC NOVELLA

Digital ISBN: 978-1-943950-43-0
Print ISBN: 978-1-943950-44-7
Edited: Fairest Reviews Editing Services
Rosa's Proofreading Services
Photographer: Wander Aguiar Photography
Cover Designer: Lori Jackson Design
Model: Jeff Burton

Ladies love the cock.

No, seriously, my road name is Rooster, and women flock to me.

The feeling's mutual, but life is too short to fall in love with anyone in particular.

I'm Vice President of the Lost Kings MC's downstate charter. There's no room in my life for distractions. Not even pretty ones.

I do who I want, when I want, and always leave them smiling.

No one's ever accused me of being a white knight. Even so, I can't resist rescuing a woman in peril.

Our paths never should have crossed.

I'm a filthy biker from New York.

Shelby's a sassy waitress from Texas.

My club's here on business. In a few days, we ride home.

Whatever secrets she's hiding aren't my problem.

If I don't believe in love, why am I falling so hard?

THE LOST KINGS MC SERIES

No other books in the series need to be read in order to enjoy Swagger and Sass but here is a complete list.

After Glow (Lost Kings MC #11)
Zero Hour (Lost Kings MC #11.5)
Zero Tolerance (Lost Kings MC #12)
Zero Regret (Lost Kings MC #13)
Zero Apologies (Lost Kings MC #14)
Swagger & Sass (Lost Kings MC #14.5)
White Lies (Lost Kings MC #15
Rhythm of the Road (Lost Kings MC #16)

Stand-Alones in the Lost Kings MC world
Bullets & Bonfires
Warnings & Wildfires
Cards of Love: Knight of Swords

Kickstart Trilogy
Kickstart My Heart
Blow My Fuse
Wheels of Fire

ACKNOWLEDGMENTS

First, I must thank authors Ryan Michele and Chelsea Camaron. If these two awesome ladies hadn't invited me into the Love, Loyalty, and Mayhem anthology earlier this year, Swagger and Sass may not even exist. LLM was an amazing adventure to take with you ladies and I'm so proud of everything we achieved.

I also need to thank some wonderful author friends who answered my distress call when I had some last minute freak-outs over the cover. Chelle Bliss, LK Shaw, Willow Winters, Kari Cole, Ginny Frost, and Cara Connelly, your willingness to answer with your thoughtful advice means the world to me. Thank you so much!

I've probably said it before, but the ladies in my FB Group are incredible. Thank you so much for all of your support, your funny comments, questions, theories and all the love and support you've shown each other. Love you!!!

Finally, thank you to Mr. Lake who is always trying to help me in any way he can and never complains about any of it.

DEDICATION

To the ones who pick us up when we're scared.

CHAPTER ONE

BIKERS PARTY WITH THE FIRE OF NONCONFORMITY ALL THE time. Rebellion. Mayhem. That's kind of our thing. While I enjoy living outside the box of civilized society, as much as any biker, even I can't see a damsel in distress and turn my back.

Both the upstate and downstate New York charters of the Lost Kings MC took the long ride down to San Antonio. We met up with two clubs we're friendly with on the way and are all staying at a ranch outside the city.

The older brothers—ones tied down with old ladies and kids—including my club president, are somewhere behind us. Sparky, Jigsaw, and I pulled ahead of the happy family pack to explore. We're charging down the narrow concrete path of the Riverwalk along the San Antonio River when I stop and hold out my arms, blocking my biker brothers, Jigsaw and Sparky, from taking another step. "What the fuck's that guy doing?"

Straight ahead and to the right, one of the walkways over the river is empty, except for some douchewaffle with a digital camera and a girl.

Sparky may be high-as-fuck, but he zeroes in on the scene in front of us fast. "Damn. Girl's dress is see-through."

Okay, maybe he didn't grasp the problem.

Yeah, Texas sun is no joke. Every inch of the girl's curvy figure is visible under the thin white dress. That's not what stopped me. Grade A tits and ass are pretty much available to me whenever I want 'em.

The jackass with the camera yells out, "Arch your back!"

"He has her move back another inch, she's going in the water," Jigsaw says, nailing the issue.

The girl hesitates and glances over her shoulder, giving me a glimpse of sun-touched cheeks and rose-red lips. "I can't swim." Nervous laughter follows her words.

Her companion rolls his eyes. "You're fine." He waves his hand in the air. "Besides, it's like ten feet deep."

2

"What an asshole," I mutter.

"Actually," Sparky says. "It's probably only two to four feet deep in this location."

As the last word leaves his mouth, the girl lets out a short yelp and tumbles backwards off the concrete bridge. Her brief scream is cut off by a loud splash.

"Shit." I push past Jiggy and Sparky, moving closer to the water. My gaze snaps to the guy peering over the edge. Isn't he going to go in after his girl?

"Brad!" she screams and flails her arms, gasping. "Help!"

"Come on, babe, it's not even that deep. Just walk to the edge." He points to the side we're standing on and laughs.

What an asshole.

Up ahead, a pair of bicycle cops seem to have taken notice of the situation.

Either it's deeper than the creep realizes, or the girl's too scared to listen. She keeps flailing and yelling in the water.

"That water's filthy. She's gonna catch beaver fever," Sparky says.

"I'm catching beaver fever right here. You can see her nipples through her wet dress," Jigsaw says.

"You're an asshole." I shrug off my cut and slap it against his chest. "Hold that." I smack Sparky's arm. "Don't let that douchebag get away. I want to have a word with him."

"Rooster, you fuckin' nuts?" Jigsaw says.

I'm already jumping into the river to go after the girl, so I ignore the question.

The water only comes up to my waist. Smells like shit and fuel oil. I reach the girl in a few quick strides. Poor thing's still thrashing and sputtering. It's cute, really.

"Calm down." I slip my arms under her and lift her in the air. "I gotcha, darlin'."

"What the? Oh!" She wraps her arms around my neck and buries her face against my chest, making it easier to carry her to the side, where my brothers are waiting and laughing their fool asses off.

"Help me, dick," I snap at Jigsaw.

He gives me a what-the-fuck look and holds out a hand to the scared girl. She ignores him and tightens her hold on me. "Sweetheart, I gotta get us out of the water." I don't like the way the cops are eyeing me. I swear to fuck if one of 'em gives me a ticket, they're gettin' a throat-punch in return.

Hesitantly, she touches her toes to the sidewalk, and Jigsaw helps her stand. I haul myself out of the water, shaking hell only knows what kind of filth off me. My water-logged jeans and boots cling in an especially uncomfortable way in the humid summer air.

"What's your name, sweetheart?" I ask.

"Shelby. Thank you," she whispers in a sweet southern drawl that perks my dick right up. Don't often hear twang like that in upstate New York.

Her scared eyes peek up at me and widen. Three six-foot-plus bikers crowding her would be too much for anyone. "Back off," I mutter to Sparky and Jigsaw.

"Shelby! Are you okay?" the photographer yells.

The asshole already earned a beating from me for letting his girl fall in the water and doing nothing to help her. But when he pushes Jigsaw out of the way to reach for her, he's risking death.

"Excuse you," Jigsaw says in the same tone of voice a serial killer might say, "Your liver will taste good with red wine and potatoes."

He didn't get the road name Jigsaw by accident.

As scary as Jigsaw can be, this is my show. That's my girl. I fished her out of the water, I get to keep her. At least for a little while. Bumping Jigsaw out of the way, I step up to this Brad asshole.

"Now's the time for you to disappear." My voice is full of cold menace meant to scare the piss out of him.

He cowers and looks around me, reaching for the girl.

Hell fucking no. "You don't listen very well, Brad."

"Got a hearing problem?" Sparky asks.

I chuckle, but it's more hollow and evil than humorous.

"Shelby, come on," Brad whispers, as if I'm not standing right in front of him. "Let's get out of here."

CHAPTER TWO

THE THREE BIKERS IN FRONT OF ME EXUDE DANGER.

Exude. That's a good one. What rhymes with it? If my notebook and pencil weren't at the bottom of the river, I'd write that down to figure out later.

Back to the bikers. I'm not in danger. Not at the moment, anyway. My lazy photographer boyfriend who couldn't be bothered to help me when I fell in the canal? He's definitely in danger.

Do I feel bad about that?

Not really.

Not when I'm soaked to the skin in slimy, smelly water. Dress ruined. Hair destroyed.

This is what I get for being cheap. Brad insisted his photos would be just as good as a professional photographer. Like an idiot, I agreed. Even though I'm scared of heights, I followed his directions. I thought it would be a cool photo.

"The fuck's wrong with you, man?" my tall, bearded savior shouts at Brad. He pushes into Brad's space, shoving him back with just the threat of his big, muscled body.

"You okay?" the tall, scruffy biker next to me asks. The way his gaze roams over my wet dress reminds me that the thin fabric is clinging to me in the most obscene way. I'm probably giving everyone in the area a good show. Uncomfortable, I cross my arms over my chest.

"Here." He shrugs off his black leather vest and yanks off his faded blue T-shirt. I'm so stunned stupid staring at the colorful ink penetrating every inch of his lean, muscled frame that I don't immediately grasp the shirt.

"Huh?" Brilliant, Shelby.

The thunder of who knows how many motorcycles passing over the street above us shakes the ground.

The corner of the biker's lip curls. "The rest of our club's not far behind. One of the girls might have something you can wear, but put that on for now."

"Right. Thank you."

Heat blooms over my cheeks. This is mortifying. The last thing I needed today. I find my way into the soft, warm shirt, noting the pungent stench of marijuana. Under that, there's a faint hint of leather and gasoline.

I finally pull the shirt into place and smile up at him. "Thank you."

He's slipped his black leather vest back on, and his gaze is trained on his biker friend who's two seconds from shoving Brad into the river.

"He your boyfriend?"

"Not anymore," I mumble.

The two remaining bikers share a look, and the one who helped us out of the water smiles down at me. There's a loud splash, and Brad goes into the river. My hero tosses the digital camera at me. "You need those shots?" he asks.

Holy crap. I can't believe he thought of that when I didn't. I quickly flip open the camera and yank out the SD card. I paid for it, so I don't suffer a lick of guilt. The camera, however, isn't mine, so I set it on the sidewalk next to where Brad's pulling himself out of the river.

"Not so funny now, is it?" I ask.

"Bitch," Brad grumbles.

I'm fixin' to pitch one hell of a hissy fit when Brad lunges at my hero. The two bikers next to me laugh. "Not too bright, is he?" one of them says.

"Not really."

"You need a ride, sugar?" the taller biker asks. He

smiles down at me again, and this time, I notice the faint, jagged scar running down his forehead to the bridge of his nose. He catches my stare, and his friendly expression turns hard.

"I think if anyone's giving her a ride, it's Rooster," the biker who donated his shirt to me says.

"Rooster?" That's my hero's name?

Wait a second, what's this guy trying to say? They're calling dibs on me?

I don't have a chance to ask. Brad charges Rooster again and gets knocked to the ground with a bone-jarring thud.

Two cops pull up on their bicycles and rush over. One grabs Rooster and throws him to the ground. "We won't tolerate your biker attitude," he growls at Rooster.

Rooster laughs.

The scarred biker is fixin' to launch himself at the cops when Rooster turns his head. "Don't, Jiggy."

"Jiggy?" I mutter.

"Jigsaw." The biker who gave me his shirt points to his friend then touches his own chest. "Sparky."

"Interesting names."

He grins at me then turns toward the cops. "Why you hassling us? This dickweed practically threw the young lady in the river. We were helping her out."

"Yeah, right." One of the cops turns and stares at me. "Shelby? Shelby Morgan?"

"Shit," I mutter.

"You famous, sweetheart?" Jigsaw asks.

The cop holds out his hand like he's calling over a reluctant cat. "Miss. Step over here, please."

I glance up at Sparky and Jigsaw. "I'm fine where I am."

The cop frowns at me.

His partner handcuffs Rooster, so now I have to do something. I can't let him get arrested for helping me. "Please don't. He really did rescue me." I turn on what I've been told is my sweet, southern charm. "I can't swim, and I was terrified." I fire a glare at Brad. "My boyfriend watched and laughed. My ex-boyfriend," I correct. "He saved me." I nod to Rooster.

"Miss Shelby, the water is only four feet deep here," the cop says, smirking at me like he thinks I'm an utter nitwit.

"I realize that *now*, officer," I answer as respectfully as I can. "But in the moment, it was scary."

He glances down at Rooster and then at his partner. "All right. Get him up."

"What's going on?" A low, commanding voice asks from behind us. I turn and yet another biker wearing the same patches these guys have is staring at us. The beautiful brunette at his side takes a step back as he drills Sparky and Jigsaw with a stare. "What did I tell you?"

My gaze skips to the patch over his heart. President.

"Uh-oh. Are you in trouble?" I whisper to Sparky.

Sparky snorts. Jigsaw laughs. "No."

"Keep your boys in line while you're in town, Prez," the first officer says with a nasty sneer.

The president ignores the attitude and nods. "I'll handle it."

The cops write out a few tickets. Two for Brad, one for Rooster, and one for me.

"I didn't go in the water on purpose!" I shout. I don't have fifty bucks let alone five hundred to pay the fine.

The cop who recognized me shrugs apologetically. "Explain it to the judge. He'll probably let it go."

Like I have time for that shit.

"You still gonna be at the Tipsy Saddle Friday night?" he asks me.

"That's why we were taking the photos." If he shows up after writing me a ticket, I'm dumping a pitcher of beer in his dang lap.

This has been the worst day.

Except for Rooster.

"Dumb bitch," Brad sneers.

"Kiss my go-to-hell!" I shoot back.

Brad hurls a few more insults at me, and the cops threaten to arrest him before he finally goes away.

"You sure you're all right, Miss Shelby?" The cop asks me, throwing plenty of stink eye at the bikers now surrounding me.

"I'm fine."

The cops take off on their bicycles, leaving me with the pack of bikers.

The biker president's patient face slips into something more disciplinary as he zeroes in on Rooster. "What'd I tell you?"

"Z, the girl went in the water. What was I supposed to do, let her drown?"

Z turns his laser blue eyes my way and smiles down at me, dimples flashing. How does this terrifying looking man actually have dimples? "You all right?"

"Yes." It takes effort to meet his commanding stare. "Rooster really did come rescue me."

He nods once. The woman at his side tugs on his hand and whispers something in his ear. "You got this?" he asks Rooster.

Rooster confirms it with a chin lift, and the pack of bikers continues along the river walk. A few hassle Rooster as they pass, but mercifully, most of them ignore me.

Rooster's gaze bounces from Sparky to Jigsaw and finally lands on me. "You need a ride, Shelby?" he asks.

"Actually, yes." Oh, shit. "My purse is in Brad's truck." Hot tears threaten to rain down my cheeks. Brad's probably long gone. He'll probably toss my purse out the window. How did my day turn to shit so dang fast?

"Let's go get it. Where'd he park?" Rooster asks.

Jigsaw's already cracking his knuckles, apparently looking forward to the confrontation.

"You can't."

Rooster cocks his head, a devilish smile playing over his lips. "Why's that?"

I wave my hands in the direction the cops rode off. "Because you barely missed getting arrested. I don't want to cause any more trouble for you."

"You're no trouble, darlin'." He glances at the stairs leading to the street level. "Where'd he park?"

"In the garage on East Houston street. But really—"

"Let's go," he says, cutting off my protest. "We're parked near there anyway."

Jigsaw and Sparky follow us as I lead the way.

"That's him!" I shout as we reach the end of the block. Like a lunatic, I point at the small silver truck about to exit the garage.

"Stay here," Rooster orders.

"No way." I reach out and grab his arm. "He's not worth it. Please don't get in trouble."

His mouth quirks. "I like you."

He extracts his arm from my hold and jerks his head toward the garage. All three of them jog over to the exit. Brad must see them because he revs the engine. He can't go anywhere because the guard hasn't lifted the gate yet.

My breath catches in my throat as Jigsaw slams his hands on the hood of the truck. Rooster walks right up to Brad's door and yanks it open.

Shouts bounce off the brick walls. Rough, angry voices drowning out Brad's pitiful protests. Brad must not give up my purse fast enough because, five seconds later, Rooster jerks my ex out of the truck and punches him. Sparky sneaks in between them and searches the front seats, emerging victorious with my green leather backpack purse raised above his head.

Rooster leans down and shares a few tense words with Brad, before releasing him and stalking away. His grim face twists into something almost apologetic when he notices me standing at the curb.

"Told you to stay over there." He almost sounds angry.

"I was worried about you."

The tension in his expression melts as he hands me my purse. "I can handle myself, sugar."

Sugar's a pretty common endearment at the bar. The guys who drop it as they're trying to peek up my dress or extract my phone number out of me are usually annoying. From Rooster, I find it charming.

Somehow, we end up holding hands. Rooster glances down as if he's surprised but not alarmed. "Let's get you home."

Butterflies stir in my stomach. Is he going to expect me to invite him in? Want some form of payment for the rescue? Will I be insulted if he doesn't?

"How long were you two together?"

"Not long." Whenever Brad kissed me, I basically zoned out. I'd go over a mental list of chores. Not even on purpose. There was no burning need or spark of desire. I can't say any of that to this man who's a stranger. This man who's making my insides melt with need by simply holding my hand. I won't admit that, either.

Just the simple, casual way Rooster swaggers down the sidewalk as if he owns the entire city is crazy-hot.

Three large, intimidating motorcycles are backed in against the curb. Rooster goes straight for the matte black one at the front of the pack.

I laugh, and he turns to me with a raised eyebrow.

"Who knew my white knight would drive a big, black Harley."

"Ride, sugar. We ride, not drive. And no one's ever accused me of being a white knight before."

So there was something special about me that made him dive into the foul river water? A thrill runs down my spine at the thought.

My gaze is drawn to the bike again. A blue and silver skull and crown decorate the gas tank. Underneath it reads, Lost Kings MC.

"Lost Kings MC. You're not from around here, are you?"

"Nope. Whole club's out on a run to strengthen the bonds of brotherhood." From someone else that might sound sarcastic, but Rooster seems genuine in his affection for his club.

"Bonding? If you're all brothers, shouldn't you already be bonded?" I knew at least a little bit from the bikers who drifted into the bar every now and then.

His smile fades. "It's been a rough year."

"I'm sorry to hear that."

"You're sweet."

Sweat rolls between my breasts, but that's not why my cheeks are so hot. It's the intense way Rooster's staring down at me making me blush. His curious eyes search my face for a moment before he touches my chin, tipping my head back. "How old are you, Shelby?" he asks in a low voice.

"Twenty-two. Why?" I stare up at him, studying his face. With the beard, it's hard to tell if he's my age or a lot older.

Instead of answering my question, he leans down and presses his lips to mine.

Fireworks.

That's the only way to describe it. There's no checking out of this kiss. I'm one hundred percent invested. His kiss does more than light a spark of desire; I'm a raging inferno of need in two seconds flat.

When he's tired of leaning over to compensate for our height difference, he doesn't break the kiss. Instead, he wraps his arms around me and lifts me up and into his body. I loop my arms around his neck, hanging on tight. My legs dangle off the ground, and I almost wrap them around his waist, but I'm still painfully aware that we're standing on a busy street in the middle of the day.

His beard is softer than I expected and tickles my chin. When I laugh, he deepens our kiss.

"That didn't take long," someone says behind us.

Rooster groans and sets me down. Keeping an arm around me, he turns to glare at Jigsaw.

I'd be embarrassed, but I really just want to keep kissing Rooster.

Jigsaw's gaze darts between Rooster and me. Asking him some silent question? Rooster gives him a subtle head shake and tightens his hold on me. Jigsaw lifts his hands as if he's surrendering.

What's up with that?

"Sparky, I need to give you back your shirt." I grasp the hem to lift it up, even though my dress is probably still see-through, but Rooster stops me.

"I'll get it later," Sparky says, with a good-natured smile. He slips on his helmet and holds out his hands, palms up. "We going or what?" he asks Jigsaw.

"Yeah." Jigsaw slaps Rooster's chest twice. "Z wants us at the table no later than six."

"Got it," Rooster growls.

"I have to work at five," I say.

"Nice meeting you, Shelby." Jigsaw grabs his helmet and nods.

The rumble from their bikes is deafening. I can't imagine what it must sound like when all three of them are fired up. Jigsaw takes off first, and Sparky follows. Rooster watches them until they turn the corner. The aggressive roar of the bikes can be heard long after they're out of sight.

My gaze strays from the direction the bikers went to

find Rooster watching me intently. "What are you doing until five?"

I tug my sticky, damp dress away from my skin. "Well, I'd like to shower and change."

The corners of his mouth quirk. "I can help you with that."

Oh, wow. My heart flutters like a hummingbird on a sugar binge. I might be in over my head here.

CHAPTER THREE

Rooster

SHELBY'S EITHER GETTING SUNBURNED, OR SHE'S SHY. SHE didn't kiss like a shy girl. But the offer to soap her up leaves her flustered.

My bad. We just met. She's not some random club girl. Offering to shower with her less than an hour after meeting might have been a bit much.

"Where are we going?" I ask.

Must not have scared her too much. She gives me the address and enough directions to find her place. "It's about seventeen minutes—"

"Seventeen, huh? That's real specific."

She blushes and unleashes that pretty smile again. "Off I-10 West. I hope it's not out of your way."

"Not at all. We're staying at a ranch off 291."

"There are a bunch of them."

Ranch probably paints the wrong picture. It's more the compound of a club we're friendly with down here. Four different clubs have taken up residence on the six hundred acre ranch this week. Hanging out. Partying. Conducting business. Strengthening alliances. Most of the officers, including me, have rooms inside the massive clubhouse. Everyone else is either bunking in a tent on the property or wherever they find room. Every night's been a party. I'd like to bring Shelby back with me. It should be calm during the day. But she's also an unpatched woman walking into a clubhouse that's housing a lot of different bikers.

"I've noticed." I reach over and grab my helmet, handing it to her. "Lot of open spaces."

"Bet you don't see that in New York."

"I'm a good hour or two above the city. We have lots of rural areas. It's just flatter here."

"We have mountains."

I chuckle. "Those are hills."

She laughs, not offended.

"Where's your helmet?"

"I'll be fine." I study her long dress and sandals. "I'm more worried about you riding in that dress and open shoes."

"I'll be okay." She glances at the bike and winces. "I think."

"I'll go easy."

That must be enough to reassure her. She eagerly climbs on behind me and wraps her arms around my middle. Feels good having her soft, warm little body hugging mine. Been a while since anyone's been back there.

"Hang on."

The sunglasses I slipped on keep most of the dust and road dirt out of my eyes. But don't do a whole lot to keep bugs from smacking into my cheeks. I take it easy through the city and open it up a bit more on the highway. Shelby's a good passenger. Moves when I move, but, otherwise, she's pretty still.

For some absurd reason, I'm jealous that she might have done this with another guy.

Her place is easy enough to find. A modest home on a postage-stamp sized piece of property. Modest might have been too generous. As I pull into the narrow, cracked driveway, I notice the yellow exterior could use a fresh coat of paint. Someone tried to cheer the place up by painting the trim a bright green. Can't say it's an improvement. Not that I'm judging. I mean, for fuck's sake, I live in a clubhouse with a bunch of bikers back home. More like a girl as sweet and pretty as Shelby should live in nicer surroundings.

Shelby braces herself on my shoulders to hop off and hands me the helmet. She's fidgety as all hell now. "It's no ranch." She waves her hand at the house. "I live with my mom."

Something about that makes me sadder.

"She home?"

"No." She stares at me for a minute then tugs on the T-shirt she's wearing. "Do you want to come in? I should probably give this to you, so you can give it to Sparky. I feel so bad he had to ride without his shirt."

"He'll be fine." Actually, he's probably fried to a crisp right about now. Fucker almost never leaves the basement. This is more sun than his pasty skin has seen in a couple years. But the more my club's been mixing with our upstate charter, the better I've gotten to know Sparky. It doesn't surprise me he'd give a girl the shirt off his back. Even if he knows damn well, he has no chance of bagging her.

And while Shelby looks damn fine in my club's colors, I can't say I care for her wearing another man's shirt. Even if it belongs to a brother and was for an emergency.

Her fidgeting only increases as we approach the front door. She slips a key out of her purse, opens the door, and steps inside. A wave of heat rolls over us, and she rushes to crank the knobs on an old window unit. It does little to cool the place off. I stop to unlace my soggy boots and leave them by the front door.

"Do you want lemonade? Iced tea?"

"Sure."

"Which one?"

"Whatever you're having."

She hesitates and glances over her shoulder. "Uh, I

was going to take a shower."

I step closer and curl my hand over her hip. "Have some tea with me first."

"Okay." She turns, and I follow her the short distance into the kitchen.

There's a small round table with four off-white chairs. I nod to the impressive line of baskets nailed along the top of the wall like some country version of crown molding. "You collect 'em?"

"No. My mom does." She grabs two glasses, setting them on the counter with a *thunk,* then moves to the refrigerator. "You want half-and-half?

"What's that?" I can't really think with her bending over in front of me.

"Half lemonade, half tea."

"Sure. I'm pretty easy to please, Shelby."

"Ugh." She sets the two pitchers on the counter and whips off her shirt.

Now I really almost lose my frickin' mind. But no, she's not getting naked for me. There's a washing machine in the kitchen, and she tosses the shirt in. "Do you want me to do yours?" she offers.

The corners of my mouth twitch. "Then I'll be shirtless."

"I was—"

I slip off my cut and drape it on the back of one of the chairs. "I'm just messing with you, Shelby."

I toss her the shirt, and she catches it midair. My jeans

are what really need the wash. As if she heard the thought, her gaze drops to my crotch, but she doesn't offer.

Pulling one of the chairs all the way out, I turn it, so I can watch her. After the laundry's started, she brings over the glasses, setting one on the table in front of me. Before she moves away, I place my hands on her hips and turn her to face me. "Thanks."

"It's the least I can do after what you did for me today. You and your friends."

"You looked terrified. I couldn't leave you."

She ducks her head. "I feel so silly now."

"Don't." I pull her closer, so she's standing between my legs, then sit upright, placing my hand at the back of her head, drawing her down for a kiss. Haven't stopped thinking about getting my mouth on hers again.

She tastes like sugar and lemons.

A soft moan drags out of her throat, and she staggers closer.

I bring my hands to her hips again, slowly sliding her dress up and encouraging her to straddle my lap, so I can keep kissing her. Fuck if she doesn't slide right into my lap like she was made for me. She presses her hot center right up against my already stiff-as-fuck cock, and I groan.

Abruptly, she pulls back. "I'm not having sex with you."

Huh. First time a girl has ever said *that* to me. "I'm just having fun kissing you right now, Shelby."

Fuck me, that's actually true.

CHAPTER FOUR

Shelby

IT'S NOT THAT I DON'T *WANT* TO HAVE SEX WITH ROOSTER. Honestly, I'm close to sliding my panties to the side, unzipping his jeans and having my way with him. Whatever he's packing behind that fly seems like it will hit the spot.

But I just broke up with my boyfriend, not even two hours ago. Sleeping with someone else so soon seems wrong.

Although, it's not like I need to worry about what Rooster thinks of me. He lives over a thousand miles away. No matter how much I like him, this can't be anything more than a fling.

Wait, I'm supposed to visit New York later this summer.

Talk about foolish. Whether or not I sleep with him, I highly doubt Rooster will even remember who I am two months from now.

All my warring thoughts ebb away as he tangles one of his big hands in my hair and pulls me down for more soft, slow kisses. "You're thinking too much, Shelby. Just be here with me."

His rough words send a shiver of desire down my spine. I cup his cheeks and throw myself into the kiss. He groans in appreciation, and his hand slides down to cup my butt, pushing me against him. The straps of my dress and bra slide down my left shoulder, and a few seconds later, Rooster traces the bare skin with his mouth, his beard tickling and igniting my skin at the same time.

He slips his finger under the other straps and whisper-soft drags them down.

"Shelby," he whispers, before kissing my neck and down my chest.

He palms one of my breasts, gently kneading. I'm hyperaware of the humid air when my nipple pops free from my bra. He wastes no time running his tongue over the stiff peak before sucking it into his mouth.

"Oh!" My fingers tighten in his hair, holding onto him or begging for more, I'm not sure.

He releases my other breast and kisses the tip.

There's a pause in sensation, and I glance down to find him studying me, palming my breast and flicking his thumb over my nipple. "You're beautiful," he rasps.

I'm no ogre, but I've never had a man admire me with such raw appreciation before either.

"Thank you." My gaze shifts and lands on a leaf and other debris stuck to my skin. I chuckle, the movement jiggling my bared breasts. "I'm a swamp thing."

"Huh?" His confused, lust-drunk eyes meet mine.

I pluck the leaf out of my cleavage and twirl it in front of his nose. "I should take that shower before we continue."

The corner of his mouth quirks up, but he doesn't suggest joining me. His restraint gives me the courage to extend the invitation.

I slide out of his lap and hold out my hand to him. "Come with me?"

He wastes no time taking my hand and standing, clearly intending to follow. As I turn, he gives me a quick tug back, capturing my attention. "You sure, Shelby?"

My heart's thudding so hard he can probably hear it. "Well, we're both pretty dirty."

Thankfully, he accepts that answer and slips his arm around my waist, resting his hand on my hip. We sort of trip into the bathroom we're so close. I push the door closed behind us with a loud click.

He raises an eyebrow as he studies the small bathtub with overhead shower.

"We'll fit," I assure him, even though I'm not sure that's true.

"It'll be tight."

"Do you want to go first?" I offer.

He frowns and shakes his head. "Fuck no." He moves to unbuckle his jeans and gives me that questioning eyebrow again.

"I can toss those in the wash for you."

"Last thing I'm worried about is my jeans, sweetheart."

Even so, I gather up his stuff and hurry out to the kitchen, tossing everything in and resetting the washer. Maybe I'm trying to give my frantic pulse a chance to slow down.

When I return, he's already in the shower.

"The hot water probably won't last long," I warn him.

He pokes his head out from behind the flowered curtain. "Better hurry then."

I gather my dress and tug it up, then stop when I realize he's still watching me. I meet his eyes, and he doesn't smile or look away. "Go on," he urges in a tone I can't resist.

I toss the dress in the sink; pretty sure it's ruined from my dip in the river.

"Hurry," he says.

I shimmy out of my panties and bra. Feeling exposed, I cross my arms over my chest. Rooster chuckles and holds out his hand. "Come here."

He pulls me into the tub with him, and his mouth automatically finds mine. It's an aggressive but welcoming kiss. He slicks his tongue along my bottom lip, and when I open my mouth, he sweeps his tongue against mine.

I moan into his mouth, and he spins us, settling me under the spray. The hot water shocks my skin, and I squeal, pushing out of his hold.

"Too hot?" he asks, reaching over to adjust the temperature.

"A little."

Bottles of shampoo, conditioner, and shower gel line the edge of the tub, and he leans over to grab one. "Get back here, so I can soap you up."

Chuckling, I gather my hair on top of my head and turn my back. Rooster's thorough, going so far as to get down on the floor of the tub to wash my legs. The firm, sudsy strokes from his hands have me ready to melt into a puddle. A tingle of excitement shoots straight between my legs when he presses his hand between my thighs.

"Turn, Shelby."

Only then do I get a full look at the big man filling up my tub. Nothing on him is small, and a tremor of fear shoots to my core.

Water raining down or not, my mouth goes dry, and my hands shake. I lean over and pick up a bottle of shampoo. "Want me to wash your beard?"

Wow, that offer was both weird and stupid.

Big, scary, bossy biker or not, Rooster's too kind to mock me.

He keeps his hands on my hips and smirks up at me. Desire shimmers in his amber eyes. "No, Shelby. I want you to *ride* my beard." He winks at me. "No helmet required."

CHAPTER FIVE

Rooster

"OH MY GOD!" SHELBY'S LAUGHTER SEEMS TO DRIVE HER fear and uncertainty away. "Does that line ever really work for you?"

"Don't know. Never used it before."

She tilts her head like she thinks I'm full of shit. But it's not a lie. I've had girls ask *me* if they could ride the beard. I've never had to offer. Shelby's all sorts of fun.

It's awkward as fuck in the tiny space, but I pull her close enough to finally get my mouth on her pussy. She's smooth and bare everywhere. Shame, I was hoping for blonde curls to match her hair, but I'm not complaining.

I hike one of her legs up and hold her, so she doesn't slip. Using my thumbs, I part her swollen lips and swipe my tongue through her wetness. Above me, she gasps and moans the second I taste her. "Hang on," I warn her.

She digs her hands into my hair, and I put my whole mouth on her, slowly licking up her center until I find her little clit.

"Oh my God," she gasps, and her knees buckle. "Rooster."

A few seconds of focused attention has her quivering and moaning so loud. My cock's screaming to get inside her, but I can be a patient man when I need to be. I want her to come hard before I impale her.

I'm also getting a vicious cramp in my neck from the awkward position. Shower sex in a space this small is bullshit. Her hips jerk, and I encourage her to grind her hot pussy against my face. Fuck, she tastes amazing. I want her juices coating my face before I'm done with her.

Keeping one hand on her hip, I give her ass a slap, and she cries out, grinding into me even harder. I keep licking and sucking until she jerks away. Breathing hard and shaking, she stares down at me.

"I've never...oh my God. Thank you."

That's what I'm talking about.

"I need a lot more of you, Shelby," I warn her as I pick myself up off the floor.

She presses her hands against my chest and slides her fingers over my skin. "Do you want to go in my bedroom?"

More than I want to breathe.

Before I have a chance to answer her or shut off the water, there's a whoosh, and a blast of cooler air hits us.

"Shelby?" a high-pitched voice calls out.

The fuck?

"Oh my, oh my," Shelby starts chanting.

"Shelby? Why is there a motorcycle in the driveway?" The voice is coming closer. There's no way the woman—who I assume is Shelby's mom—can't see me. My head sticks out above the top of the shower. Something, Shelby seems to realize as she urges me to duck down.

"Too late for that, sweetheart," I whisper, thoroughly amused at the situation.

"Shelby? Oh my God!" her mom screeches as she must finally realize her daughter isn't alone. "Are you okay?"

"I'm fine, Mom." Shelby's voice is barely more than a squeak.

The door slams shut.

Shelby slaps her hands over her face. "I'm so sorry," she mutters.

I almost answer, 'Not the first time something like that's happened,' but it feels like a shitty thing to say for some reason. Instead, I pry her hands away from her face. "You're twenty-two. Never had a guy over before?"

"No, I have. Just not...nothing like this ever. Oh my God. I'm so sorry."

"Stop apologizing. It's not a big deal." I glance over my shoulder. "Unless she's going for a shotgun or something." This is Texas after all.

35

Finally, she laughs. "No shotgun."

The water starts to cool. Whether we've exhausted the hot water tank or it's the mom's way of forcing us out of the shower, I'm not sure. Either way, it does nothing to cure my raging hard-on.

"Rooster," she whispers, wrapping her fingers around my dick. "I wanted to take care of you."

I suck in a quick hit of air. Her little fingers feel amazing. "Keep stroking, baby."

She gives me a wicked smile then drops to her knees. Guess she forgot her mom's right outside. Not that I'm complaining.

Her soft, wet tongue flicks against the underside of my cock. "Oh, fuck. This won't take long."

She peeks up at me and presses a finger to her lips. "Shhh."

"I'll do my—"

My words are lost as she swoops in and wraps her lips around my cock, sliding down as far as she can. She curls her hand around what she can't fit in her mouth and gives a nice counter twist. "Fuck," I groan.

Bracing one hand on the wall and the other on the back of her head, I pump my hips a few times. I'm so erratic and out of control, she ends up resting her hands on my hips and letting me have my way with her mouth.

"Shelby, fuck. That's it." At the last minute, I yank my dick out of her mouth and shoot cum all over her wet tits.

"Thank you," she whispers.

It wasn't politeness that stopped me from shooting down her throat. It was the desire to see my cum painting her beautiful body. But I'm thoroughly spent, so I just nod and brush my knuckles against her cheek. "You okay?"

She nods, and I help her stand, turning her to face the water, so I can reluctantly clean her off.

Washing turns to groping and a few seconds later, I'm pinching her little nipples and turning her head, so I can kiss her again. She grinds her ass into my half-hard cock, and I groan. I haven't had enough of her yet.

"Shelby!" Someone bangs on the bathroom door. Right. Forgot about the scandalized mom out there.

"Shoot." Shelby pulls away and slams the water off. "I'm so sorry," she whispers to me.

"It's okay."

We climb out, and she tosses a towel at me. Fuck, I forgot she took my clothes and washed them.

Shelby seems to have the same thought. Her lips twist with remorse. "I'm so sorry. I probably have a pair of gym shorts or something..."

"I'm fine." Got nothing to hide. I mean, it's not like her mom didn't just hear her daughter giving me head. Might as well go for full-throttle awkward and parade around the house in a towel that barely hides my balls.

Thankfully, her mom's not waiting outside the bathroom door for us.

Something awful occurs to me, and I grasp Shelby's

arm, stopping her in her tracks. "You *are* twenty-two, right?"

She lets out a soft laugh. "Yes." She points to the right. "My bedroom, if you'd rather wait there."

I'm not going to wait in there like a pussy, but I do follow her in while she gets dressed. The gym shorts she has for me must have belonged to a high school boyfriend because they wouldn't fit my arm, let alone my anywhere else.

"Sorry," she says again. "I'll get your stuff in the dryer."

"Hey." I stop her and push her wet, tangled hair off her shoulder. "Stop apologizing." I search her face. "You embarrassed to introduce me to your mom?"

"No. God, Rooster. Not at all."

"Good."

She slips into this short, loose black dress. I almost lose my damn mind when she slides a tiny black thong underneath.

Still wearing the towel, I follow her into the kitchen where an older, plumper, just-as-pretty version of Shelby paces back and forth. "Oh my God! Shelby, are you okay!?"

"I'm fine."

The woman's gaze lands on me then returns to her daughter.

Shelby's cheeks turn pink. "This is my friend, Rooster."

"Rooster?"

I hold out my hand. "Nice to meet you, Mrs. Morgan."

The lady narrows her eyes and quickly shakes my hand.

"I thought you left with Brad this morning," she asks Shelby. By the tone she uses to say Brad's name, I'm guessing she's not a fan.

"I did." Shelby rests her hip against the counter, and feeling protective, I place my hands on her shoulders. "He wanted to take these stupid photos at the Riverwalk. I fell in the water."

"Oh, baby," her mom coos. "You can't swim."

"I know." Shelby shrugs. "Brad thought it was hysterical. But I was scared to death." She turns and nods at me. "Rooster jumped in the water and carried me out."

Mom's suspicious hawk eyes are softer when they land on me again. "You did?"

I shrug. "She sounded terrified. I couldn't leave her in there."

"Well, thank you." Her lips quirk as she pulls Shelby against her for a hug. "You could've thanked him with dinner, you know."

"Mom," Shelby protests. "We were all gross from the river water."

Her mom laughs and releases Shelby. "Sure, honey." Her gaze skips to my towel, and she raises an eyebrow at me.

"Your daughter took my clothes hostage, Mrs. Morgan."

"You can call me Lynn." She gestures at the washing

machine. "I think it's done. Better get his stuff in the dryer if you want to get to work on time, Shelbs."

Shelby drags herself away from both of us and busies herself pulling stuff out of the washer and plopping it into the dryer.

"That bike yours?" Lynn asks.

"Yup."

"Got New York plates."

"I'm visiting the area."

"Uh-huh." Suspicious mom returns. She nods at my leather cut still draped over one of the dining room chairs. "Your whole MC down here?"

"Yeah, we're friendly with the local club. It's all good."

She breathes out a sigh of relief. "Okay, I just don't want her..."

"No one will bother her, Lynn."

The fear vanishes from her eyes. She tilts her head and studies me. "You're nicer than I'd expect."

Meaning she's had some bad run-ins with bikers. "I have my moments." I wink at her. "And a weakness for pretty ladies."

Flirting seems to work. She opens the refrigerator and offers to feed me. Shelby's jaw drops. Maybe Lynn's not usually so polite to Shelby's boyfriends, but in Brad's case, I kind of don't blame the woman.

Shelby fusses with setting the table and pouring tea while her mother fixes lunch. As Shelby backs away, I reach out and grab her hand. "Hey, you okay?"

Her nervous eyes meet mine. "I'm sorry, I'm basically holding you hostage here."

I laugh and lean in to kiss her forehead. "Baby, if I wanted to go, I'd go. Pants or not."

She chuckles, and some of the tension seems to drain out of her. "Okay."

Her mother sets out heaping portions of chicken fried steak, mashed potatoes, and green beans. Shit, I think I'm in love with this family.

"Leftovers from the diner," Lynn says, almost as an apology.

"Looks great to me. Thank you." It's been an eventful day, and I'm starving.

"Shelby?" Lynn's voice is low as if she's hoping I won't notice. But we're all in pretty tight quarters. Even so, I keep my face focused on my plate.

"You and Brad?" she prompts her daughter.

"O-V-E-R." Shelby sighs. "He was such a jackass."

"Boy was born on third and always thought he hit a triple," Lynn mutters. Damn, I like this lady. "Dickless wonder, too."

Now I see where Shelby gets her sass from.

Shelby snorts. "We got the photos, though. Rooster saved the SD card for me."

"Good." They're both quiet, and I look up to see them sharing some sort of silent communication. Shelby shrugs and shakes her head.

As we're finishing up, my phone buzzes. I flick the

screen and check the texts from Jiggy. "Damn," I mutter.

"Do you have to go? One of your friends said you were meeting...are you late?"

"Nah, it's okay." Actually, that's not true. Z needs me at this meeting, and after everything he's done to keep our charter together and the faith he's put in me by nominating me for Vice President, I don't want to disappoint him. Shelby seems to sense my inner conflict and leans over to yank open the dryer door.

"Your stuff's almost finished."

"Thanks."

She hands me the bundle of clothes, and I head to her bedroom to change.

CHAPTER SIX

Shelby

"IT TAKES AN AWFULLY CONFIDENT MAN TO EAT A MEAL IN A towel in a stranger's house," my mother says, when I return to the kitchen.

I laugh and shrug. "I guess."

"You seem to like him."

"I do." I shrug again, not quite comfortable discussing this with my mother, when Rooster's in the other room.

"Fine looking man, too." Her gaze darts to the hallway.

"Hands off, Mom."

She laughs and starts clearing the table. "Don't worry, sweetheart. I still like my men more seasoned."

Rooster's plenty seasoned. I swear my legs are still jelly from the orgasm he gave me before. I've never come so hard in my life.

"Are you going to invite him to—"

"Hell, no. He's only here for a few days. He doesn't want to go to some hillbilly bar—"

"Shelby." She sighs and shakes her head. "Baby, you're so talented. How much more do you need to accomplish before you believe it?"

I raise my hands and sweep my gaze over our tiny rental house. "Getting us out of here would help."

"That's not your job, honey."

Shit, I didn't mean to make my mother feel bad. She's been struggling to provide for both of us since my dad walked out more than a decade ago. She's sacrificed a lot to help me achieve my dreams. "You've done enough. It's time for me to take care of you."

She wraps me up in a comforting hug. "You're doin' fine, and I have faith in you."

"Thanks."

The floor creaks as Rooster enters the kitchen. "I'm sorry, Shelby. I really do need to go. Do you need a ride to work or anything?"

"No, my Mom will take me."

My mother—meddler that she is—elbows me, but I ignore it. "I'll walk you out, though."

He stops by the door to lace up his boots, and I admire his long, dexterous hands. He'd be a great piano player. "Do you play any instruments?" I blurt out.

He doesn't even blink at the out-of-nowhere question. "Nope. No musical talent whatsoever."

"Hmm. Shame. You have great hands."

One corner of his mouth twitches, and he pulls me closer. "Didn't get to put them on you enough to satisfy me."

"Oh no?"

"No."

We stare at each other for a few minutes. "Come outside with me."

When we reach his bike, he leans against the seat and pulls me between his legs. "When can I see you again?"

Surprised, and maybe a little suspicious, I don't answer right away. "How long are you here?"

"A week or so, but I can rearrange some things and stay longer."

Rearrange them, how? "Don't you have a job back in New York?"

There's that sexy half-smile again. "Yeah, but it's a make-up-my-own hours sort of situation."

"Oh."

"This trip is part business, too."

"Oh," I say again. Apparently, words are too complicated.

"You working tonight?"

"Until midnight."

"At the Tipsy Saddle?"

Surprised he remembered, I blink before answering. "Ah, no. That's uh, my side job."

"What's your main job?"

"Waitressing. Same place my mom works."

"You get to eat chicken fried steak like that every night?" he teases.

I poke my stomach. "Hell, no. I have enough padding."

He rolls his eyes. "Your perfect body is forever burned in my mind, Shelby."

I lean in and run my fingers over his stomach. "Same here."

He makes this sexy growly noise and leans in to kiss me. When he pulls back, he searches my face for a few seconds. "That cell phone in your bedroom yours?"

"Uh, yeah. Why?"

"I got your number. And you've got mine. We're having a big party this weekend. I'd like you to come if you're interested."

"Yeah. Sure."

"Don't get too excited. It'll be outdoors."

"That's okay."

He leans in and kisses my forehead. "I'm free later tonight if you want to call me when you get off work."

"Okay," I whisper.

The pavement vibrates under my feet when he fires up his bike. Even the way he carefully backs the big machine out of my driveway is sexy as hell to witness.

Watching him go leaves an ache inside I've never quite felt before.

CHAPTER SEVEN

Rooster

"Look who decided to show up!" Jigsaw calls out, as soon as he sees me.

"Shut up, dick," I grumble, not wanting him to draw attention to my late arrival.

"Bro, Blaise pushed the meeting back. You're good."

"Why didn't you tell me?" I could've spent more time with Shelby if I wasn't so worried about missing this meeting.

"I just found out." He lifts his chin. "Z's waiting for you, though."

"Fucking great." I turn, and Z is, indeed, outside. But he's busy with his old lady and his kid, so I don't think he's real worried about my whereabouts.

There's a scraping noise behind me, and someone

tackles me from behind. By the size and chokehold, I assume it's Murphy. "Don't make me break your ass in front of your wifey and daughter," I warn him.

"Heard you played hero this morning." He releases me and slaps my back a few times.

I roll my eyes at Jigsaw. "Can't you keep your mouth shut?"

"Wasn't me. Sparky told everyone."

Whatever. It's impossible to be pissed at our stoner brother. "I got his shirt. Where is he?"

"You fuck her?" Jigsaw asks.

"Shut up," I grumble.

"Sounds like a *no*." Murphy laughs.

I flip him off. "Don't you have your own girl to worry about?"

"I'm not the one who asked. Don't really care where you stick your dick."

Jigsaw slaps Murphy's arm. "She was hot. Had nice round little titties—"

"Shut the fuck up," I snap.

Murphy rolls his eyes at Jiggy. "Why you gotta be a dick?"

"Oh, sorry. You marrying her or something?" Jigsaw asks, without a note of remorse in his voice.

"No, asshole." I pause to consider whether I should tell Jigsaw this. I'm sure as fuck not interested in his opinion. "I invited her up Saturday, though."

"Why? There's going to be so much free pussy—"

"Worry about your own dick, would ya?"

He rubs his cheek and gives me a sly half-smile. "She up for a spit roast?"

"You looking to die today?"

"Brother must be tired of his guts being on the inside," Murphy says.

Jigsaw grins. "Jealous, Ginger?"

"Nope. I got all I need right over there." He nods at his fiancée who's busy playing with her daughter and Z's son while talking to Z's old lady.

"Upstate's going to infect our charter with monogamy, brother." Jigsaw slaps his hand against my chest. "It's up to *us* to stop the spread of that disease."

"For fuck's sake," Murphy mutters. "You and Ravage really need to hang out more."

"You act like I'm patching her and taking her back to New York with me." Although, now that the words are out of my mouth, I can't shake the idea of having her back home with me out of my head.

"She got any hot sisters you can bring Saturday?" Jigsaw asks.

"I don't think so. She lives with her mom."

"Her mom hot?"

"Jesus Christ."

"What? Age ain't nothin' but a number, bro. I don't discriminate."

"Tell me, is your ass jealous of the shit that comes out of your mouth?" Murphy asks.

I snort and give him a fist bump before answering Jiggy's question. "Yeah, she could be Shelby's older sister."

"Bring her."

"Yeah, I'll put that at the top of my list."

"Cock-a-doodle-doo!" someone yells out right before something soft hits me in the back of the head.

"What the fuck?" I bend down and pick up the bundle of koozies Ravage tossed my way. They're neon pink and have three symbols printed on the front: an eye, a heart, and a rooster. "The fuck is this?"

LOST KINGS MC

"I love cock," Ravage answers, sounding out each syllable like he's talking to a moron. "For the party."

I vaguely remember talking about this with him before we left New York. At the time, it seemed like a funny idea. Hand them out to chicks, then go up and tell them my name's Rooster. Something stupid like that. I was probably high when Ravage brought it up.

When I don't show the proper amount of enthusiasm, Ravage snatches the package out of my hands. "Ingrate. More for me."

"If we weren't in the middle of fucking nowhere," Murphy mutters, "Heidi and I would've stayed at a hotel."

Ravage shoves Murphy to the side. "Fuck you, bro. You got a nice cushy room in the fancy part of the ranch."

"It's Dad alley down there." Jigsaw shakes his head. "Nothing but our fallen, castrated brothers. We don't want to be anywhere near there."

Murphy clasps his hands under his beard prayer style. "Please say that to Rock's face and let me know how it works out for you."

Ravage taps his chin. "Our prez is likely to gut a motherfucker for even *looking* at his wife."

"She's quite MILF-y, so I get it," Jigsaw says.

"Bro, you need to go rub one out before we sit down?" I slap Jigsaw's chest. "You seem awfully one-track minded today."

"Nah, Lala sucked me dry when we got back."

"Way too much info."

Ravage scowls at me as if he'd planned to ask for details.

"You fuck Shelby or not?" Jigsaw asks.

"None of your business."

"You did, didn't you? Was she a firecracker?"

"Shut up."

Murphy shakes his head in disgust. "I'll see you at the table."

Ravage watches Murphy talk to Lilly for a minute, then drags Heidi into the house. "Teller's been bitching all day that their room is right next to his." He laughs. "Should be an eventful afternoon."

"Christ, I feel like I walked into a fucking soap opera," I grumble.

"Lost Kings MC: Road Trip Season." Ravage spreads his arms out wide. "It's awesome."

Chuckling, I slap his shoulder and make my way over to Z.

"Hey, hero." He grins at me. "Everything go okay?"

"Eh, got a ticket from the cops."

"Get the girl home all right?"

My mouth curves up. "Yeah, she's nice. Thinking of having her up on Saturday."

He nods and searches the grounds. "Keep an eye on her. We got a lot of out-of-town bikers here we don't know. Couple different clubs."

"I will," I promise. "I heard Blaise pushed back the meeting?"

"Yeah, he had something going on. Dante's supposed to call everyone when they're ready."

Only the officers of each club would be sitting down at the big meeting. Then each club will discuss the details of what went down. More efficient. First time we've ever done this. It'll be good for all four organizations if we can make it work.

Give us easy passage and alliances throughout a huge portion of the country. All of us want it to go smoothly.

When we all finally sit down, it's clear Lost Kings have the best operation. Yeah, I'm biased, but we do. Upstate has their weed operation. They run that shit tight.

Sparky's the genius behind their grow-op. Downstate, we have our porn studio that brings in the majority of our cash. Some other side ventures, too, but they have nothing to do with this meeting.

Iron Bulls MC runs narcotics and probably guns down to Mexico. Devil Demons MC runs narcotics into Canada. Savage Dragons MC—I'm not really clear what the fuck they do. But they're a close ally of the Iron Bulls, and one of them owns this ranch, so that's how they ended up here. While my club has no interest in the heavier end of the criminal spectrum, we want to keep relationships with these clubs running smoothly. Sparky's been helping the Iron Bulls set up their own grow operation, and he goes into a lengthy lecture about strains and growing techniques that puts most of us to sleep.

My treasurer, Hustler, lays out some details about the porn proposal we put together. We held some stuff back, naturally. Kings first and all that. Iron Bulls have some connections to talent in California that we want, and we work out a deal on that.

Once business finishes, it's time to party.

And I'm wondering if there's any way Shelby can get off work a little early.

CHAPTER EIGHT

Shelby

I'M FEELING LIKE TEN MILES OF BAD ROAD WHEN I CLOCK IN at the diner. A steady stream of customers comes and goes all night. Even so, my shift seems to drag on and on.

Rooster: You never told me where you work?

Me: Is your meeting over already?

I shove my phone back in my apron pocket and finish placing the giant five-pound cinnamon roll on a plate before carrying it over to one of my tables.

After another lap around the room, refilling coffees and clearing empty plates, I finally have a second to text Rooster back.

Me: Auntie Eclair's diner.

It's too far out of his way to worry about seeing him tonight.

Two hours later, I realize my assumption was dead wrong. The parking lot vibrates with the rumble of dozens of motorcycles. Okay, dozens might be stretching it, but there are a lot of them pulling up.

Customers glance out the windows and cast nervous glances around.

Rooster walks in the door first and smiles as soon as he sees me.

I recognize Jigsaw and Sparky from earlier, but at least ten more don't-fuck-with-me type of men wearing leather vests crowd in behind them.

"Hey." I rush over and greet Rooster. "Give me a second to put enough tables together for you."

"We can do it." He nods to an empty section in the back of the diner. "That okay?"

"Perfect."

He pats my shoulder and stalks past me. Jigsaw nods as he passes. "Evening, Shelby."

Sparky stops in front of me. "Tell me there are more of those cinnamon buns."

"Yup. Got at least a dozen fresh ones in the back."

"Bring *all* of them to us."

"They're like fifteen dollars apiece."

He smirks as if he's insulted. "Coffee, too," he adds, before following his brothers.

The rest of the guys nod at me as they go by. I'm too flustered to bother reading their patches and learning their names. I do notice that not all of them belong to the same club as Rooster. They all seem friendly and familiar with each other. *That's a good sign, right?*

My manager steps out and assesses the room. "Friends of yours?"

"Sort of. Well, one of them is."

"Make sure it stays civil."

Yeah, because a bunch of beefy bikers give a damn what I have to say about anything. "Of course."

Positive Sparky was kidding, I only bring two of the cinnamon buns to the table. He makes sad puppy eyes at me. "Where's the rest of them?"

"Are you sure?"

He glances at them again. "Box up the rest, we'll take 'em home."

One of his brothers slaps his shoulder. "Wrath will kill you if you bring all that sugar back."

Sparky shrugs. "We're on vacation."

One of the other bikers pipes up, "I wouldn't need sugar either if I was married to a sweet piece of ass like his wife."

Sparky shoots a glare down the table.

I rest my hand on Rooster's shoulder. "Couple pots of coffee for the table?"

"That'd be perfect."

"Thanks, darlin'," someone else calls out.

It takes forever to get everyone their coffee, water, and other drinks. I'm praying no one wants any real food because the kitchen is almost shut down. But they seem content with the cinnamon buns and coffee.

About a quarter to midnight, Rooster and Jigsaw get up and do a lap around the restaurant, eyeing my straggling customers in an unfriendly way.

"You trying to slash my tips in half tonight?" I whisper, when he stops by the counter.

"We'll take care of you, sweetheart."

"I don't need charity, Rooster."

"You've earned every penny taking care of a big party like ours right at the last minute."

He says it in a sweet way that doesn't make me feel like he looks down on me for being a waitress. "Thanks."

He leans his elbows on the counter. "You need a ride home?"

The low rumble of his voice suggests he has more than dropping me off at home in mind. "I have my mom's car." If I'd known he was stopping in, I would've walked the seven miles here. "But she's out tonight if you want to come over and watch a movie or something." A movie sounds safe. I mean, I can't openly invite him over for sex, right?

"I have to be up early for my other job," I add. Technically, it's a rehearsal, but I don't know how to say that without inviting questions I'm not ready to answer.

His mouth turns down as if he's disappointed. "You work two jobs?"

Maybe he's more concerned about how hard I have to

hustle. "Sort of. More when I can." I shrug. "I try to help out my mama as much as I can."

"I get that." He places his warm hands over mine, drawing them closer. "Sure you're not too tired? You've had an exciting day."

Exhaustion tugs at me, but I grab his beard and give it a gentle tug. "You did offer me a ride earlier."

His sensual lips curl into a panty-dropping smile. "I sure did, sugar."

CHAPTER NINE

Rooster

I'M RAPIDLY BECOMING ADDICTED TO THIS GIRL.

How could I not? She's sweet as hell. Sassy sometimes. Shy other times. A whole bunch of contradictions I really enjoy.

"Let me guess, you're not coming back to the clubhouse with us tonight," Jigsaw says, when I take my place at the table again.

"Fuck off." I'm really not in the mood to be ribbed by my brothers anymore tonight. I'd wanted to get to the diner earlier, but it'd been like herding turtles to get these guys on the road.

"You realize we got plenty of ass back at the clubhouse, right?" Hammer asks. He's a member of the Savage Dragons MC. If I'd known he was going to be so obnoxious, I wouldn't have invited him along on this four club bonding activity Z suggested.

Shelby returns to the table with four huge white pastry boxes and sets them in front of Sparky. "That's everything I've got back there."

"Cool. Thanks, Shelbs."

"How're you planning to get those back?" Ravage asks.

Sparky shrugs. "We can each take one."

The guys at the end of the table rumble with laughter. "I'll call a prospect down," Blaise offers.

I let them deal with the logistics of transporting Sparky's munchies and go find Shelby.

IT SEEMS like hours until she's finally able to leave. Poor girl's dead on her feet. "You sure you're up for company?"

"Yes. Unless you don't want to…"

"I want to," I assure her. Can't remember the last time I wanted a girl this much. "I'll follow you home."

She nods, but before she slips into her car, I pull her to me and slam my mouth over hers. She gasps and wraps her arms around my neck, going up on her tiptoes to get closer to me. Pushing her back against her car, I lift her, so she's at the perfect height. My hands slide up under her dress, gripping her ass.

"I'm wide awake now," she whispers.

"Good."

I set her down and hold her door open, shutting it only after she's safely tucked inside. She quickly rolls the window down. "You remember where it is in case we get separated?"

"I'll be right on your ass, don't worry."

She reaches out and takes my hand for a brief second. "Okay."

The ride to her house has to be the longest fifteen minutes of my life.

While she invited me over under the pretense of watching a movie, I never give her the chance to flick on the television.

Once we're inside, I pin her to the front door, lifting her the way I'd done in the parking lot. "You sure your mom won't walk in on us again?"

"Ninety-five percent sure."

"Good enough for me."

"Rooster?"

"Yeah?" I slide her purse off her shoulder and drop it on the bench next to the door. After taking one more taste of her lips, I carry her to the bedroom.

"Uh, remember I said I didn't want to have sex earlier?"

I stop cold right outside her bedroom door. "Uh-huh."

Her fingers twist in my hair. "Well, I, uh, kinda changed my mind."

"Jesus, woman. You trying to give me a heart attack?"

She giggles and starts unbuttoning the top of her

dress. I set her down and close her bedroom door. Thank fuck there's a lock, because I flick that too. "Just in case."

She laughs some more and tosses her dress in the direction of an overflowing hamper. "Sorry for the mess."

"I couldn't give a fuck. I'm only interested in you, Shelby." My hungry eyes sweep over every exposed inch of her. Really digging the sexy black lace bra that gives me a glimpse of her sweet pink nipples. "God damn, you're sexy."

"Thank you." She curls her index finger, calling me to the bed. It's a double bed. Small, but doable. Fuck, I think I'd fuck her on the floor right about now if that was my only option.

She slides my cut off and gently places it on her desk. I like the way she knows to treat it with care and not just toss it aside.

"Come here." I cup her cheeks with my hands and lean down to take her lips. Her eager little hands slide up under my shirt, pushing it up. "Eager much?" I tease, taking it off and tossing it on the desk.

"Yes. I've been turned on all afternoon. I thought I was going to explode when you swaggered into the diner tonight."

Shit, there's something really sweet about that. No games or coy hesitation. But she's not overly aggressive like a club girl on the prowl either.

Her hands skim around the waistband of my jeans, and I work the belt loose.

"Rooster?"

"Yeah?"

"What's your name? Your real name," she clarifies.

"Who says it's not Rooster?"

She glances at the bed. "I just—"

I get it. She doesn't want to sleep with someone whose name she doesn't know. Can't remember the last girl I was with who gave a shit about stuff like that. "Logan. Logan Randall."

"Logan. I like that."

Stripped down to my boxer briefs now, I stretch out on her bed. "Come get your ride, little girl." She laughs. "There's nothing little about me."

"Next to me there is. Now get up here." I sit up and grab her hand, dragging her onto the bed. She kneels next to me and traces her fingers down my chest.

"Are you sure?"

"About wanting that pretty pussy of yours in my face? Fuck yeah, I am."

She chuckles again. Really love the sound of her laugh.

I hook my fingers in her little black panties. "Take these off for me."

She wiggles out of them and also stops to unhook her bra.

"Fuck." I scrub my hand over my face. "How are you even hotter than I remember?"

Instead of answering, she grips my cock through my

shorts. "I'm wondering if I imagined how big this monster really is."

"Go ahead and verify."

She works my briefs down my legs, and my cock springs up, excited to see her again.

"Rooster," she whispers, using both hands to stroke up and down my shaft. Leaning over, she takes me in her mouth, and my hips jerk.

"Fuck." My fingers tangle in her hair. This wasn't quite how I saw things going, but I'm certainly not complaining.

She keeps up the sweet torture until I'm ready to blow.

"Stop. Stop. Get up here."

CHAPTER TEN

Shelby

I SWIPE MY HAND OVER MY LIPS. "YOU TASTE GOOD." MAYBE that's a weird thing to say, but I can't help it. Rooster doesn't seem to mind.

The intensity in his eyes ratchets up another notch. "Climb on up here."

The pleasure he'd given me earlier was so intense, that a tremor of fear runs through me. Not enough to turn him down. Just enough to make my heart beat faster.

He guides me up over his chest. Flexing his sinfully sculpted arms, he lifts me until I'm hovering over his face. "That's it. Come to me," he encourages.

The first touch of his tongue against my flesh is a jolt of electricity to my system. "Uh," I gasp, my hips jerking forward.

He hums an encouraging noise, and I brace my hands against the wall.

After that, it's game on. He's completely focused on licking, kissing, and tasting every inch of me. Not just my core. He stops to take soft nibbles and licks of my inner thighs, my mound. No portion of me is left untouched. All my nerve endings fire up, leaving me trembling and close to orgasming again.

"Rooster." My voice comes out with a desperate, breathy urgency.

He makes some encouraging noises that sound like *come.* Maybe I'm too wound up from today, but my orgasm remains just out of reach, no matter how much pressure he applies to my clit. Finally, he slips two fingers inside me, and I shudder with relief. He keeps sucking at my clit while I grind myself against his face. His beard tickles my thighs, adding to the flood of sensations.

"Rooster, I'm—" The rest of my words are lost to crying and moaning in relief. "Oh my God," I mutter over and over.

"Shelby," he rasps, voice raw with desperation. "Need you on my dick, sugar."

"God yes." I shimmy down his body, eager for more, then stop. "Do you have condoms?"

He lifts up, and I admire the flex and ripple of his stomach muscles. "Jeans."

"Good, I don't think the ones I have will fit you."

He falls back on the bed laughing as I snag the jeans and yank the little foil squares out of his pocket. I hand one to him, and he flips me on my back. After rolling the condom on, he kisses his way up my body, stopping to lick and nibble spots that make me writhe under him. Finally, he straddles my hips.

I'm so wet and eager, I shamelessly spread my legs wide. Doesn't stop him from teasing me by dragging his cock up and down my slit a few times.

"Logan, please."

A shift of his hips lines us up perfectly. With agonizing slowness, he sinks inside. We fit together so right. A tight fit. But perfect. We both groan, and his lips meet mine. His hips keep rolling at that teasing, slow pace designed to drive me wild.

Heat races over every exposed inch of my skin. He twines his fingers with mine and pulls my arms over my head. With one hand, he pins my wrists to the bed. He clutches my hip with his free hand and drives into me harder.

I've never experienced anything like this before. There's this amazing physical connection. But something else bubbles below all our explosive chemistry.

My nerve endings tingle and sizzle. I'm close to going off again. He accelerates, hooking his arm behind my knee. "Fuck me back, Shelby," he whispers against my lips.

I buck against his thrusts and gasp at the swelling pleasure.

"That's a girl. Harder," he encourages.

He rams into me with such force, I'm sure I'll splinter apart. At the last second, he captures my gaze. The steady eye contact pushes me over the edge again. He groans and thrusts harder, letting out a stream of beautiful curses as he explodes inside me.

He keeps moving and groaning and finally slows his frantic movements. He drops his forehead to my chest and places a kiss between my breasts.

"You're unreal, Shelby," he murmurs.

Carefully, he holds the base of the condom and slips free. "Give me a second."

Too content to speak, I watch him go. After a minute, I jump up and use the bathroom. He's returning from the kitchen with a glass of water when I open the door.

"I was worried you left."

He scowls. "Not fucking likely." He stays rooted to the spot, his gaze roaming over my nude body.

"You're more beautiful than I deserve."

I take the water and sip slowly before answering. "I doubt that."

"You all right with me staying?" He follows me back to my room.

I scoot to the side of the bed against the wall to make room for him. "I'll be offended if you don't."

He snaps off the lamp on my nightstand and stretches out next to me. "Come here."

Our breaths mingle together, and within seconds, I'm out cold.

CHAPTER ELEVEN

Rooster

STEADY THUMPS AND SHOUTS PULL ME FROM SLEEP.
Shelby's soft, warm naked body is still sprawled out
against me. I allow my hands to wander over her curves
for a few seconds before noticing the ruckus outside
again.

What the fuck?

Afraid whoever it is will wake her, I reach down and
snatch up my jeans.

"Rooster?" Her morning rough voice is sexy-as-fuck,
and I'm ready to pin her down and fuck her speechless
again.

"I think someone's at your door."

She wrinkles her nose and glances at the clock.
"Shoot, I never set my alarm. I'm late."

"For?" I ask, letting the question hang.

Again, she's squirrely about telling me her plans. Maybe she's a stripper and she's embarrassed? But I don't get that vibe from her. Plus, she doesn't seem to own anything with glitter or sequins on it.

Tipsy Saddle. Isn't that where one of the cops said she'd be tonight? Sounds like a bar. Maybe she's a topless waitress? Certainly, has the tits for the job.

Guys would be tripping over themselves to get at her.

Fuck, the idea of beating guys off her heats my blood.

The pounding on the front door starts up again. I stalk out to the living room and yank open the door.

The douchebag I didn't punch nearly enough yesterday, Brad, is on the other side. He recoils the second he sees me.

"Where's Shelby?"

"Not your concern."

"Brad?" Shelby yells. "What are you doing here?"

"You fucking slut! Took me two months to pry open your legs, but you're fucking this guy—"

I cut off his insults by wrapping a hand around his neck, choking off his air supply. "Say one more word to her, and I'll snap your motherfucking head off. We clear?"

He nods once and gasps. His hands claw at my arm, but I'm not done.

"You two are *over*. You stop by, call her, do anything to bother her ever again, I'll fucking end you."

His head moves a millimeter or two. I'm grasping too tight for him to nod properly. "Yes," he gasps.

"Good." I throw him to the ground, and he crab crawls away a few feet before standing.

His lips part to throw more nasty words at Shelby and I'm right up in his face again. "Do it and I'll beat you to death on her front lawn."

Finally, he holds his hands up in surrender. "I'm going."

I wait and watch him leave before going back inside.

"Thank you," Shelby whispers. "I'm sorry."

"What are you sorry for? He's the asshole."

She shrugs.

"You need a ride?"

"No. I called and let them know I'm running late. Come inside so I can make you breakfast." She leans up and kisses my cheek. "I at least owe you some eggs after all those magnificent orgasms you gave me."

"Magnificent, huh?" I slam the door behind us and follow her into the kitchen.

CHAPTER TWELVE

Shelby

THIS MORNING, ALL THE LIGHTS ARE BLAZING INSIDE THE Tipsy Saddle. Somehow, the interior is still dark and shadowy. The scent of stale popcorn and spilled beer lingers in the air. A pungent, sweaty aroma will get added to the mix tonight when the place is packed with our regular buzzed two-stepping crowd.

"I'm so sorry!" I yelp, as I hurry inside and set down my guitar.

Trent's waiting in the long hallway and leans down to grab my guitar case. "You're never late. Everything okay?"

Beyond him, I make out the dull wooden bar with a line of stools neatly nestled underneath. No matter how many times we clean that bar top, it's always a bit sticky.

Beyond that, chairs are neatly stacked on top of scarred wood tables. A hearty layer of sawdust coats the floor.

As far as honky-tonks go, it's not the worst I've ever visited.

"Broke up with Brad," I admit.

"Bout time. He ain't worth two cents, Shelby. Never was good enough for ya."

Yeah, the few times I'd brought Brad to rehearsal, he'd managed to alienate every person he came into contact with. Even Trent, who's the most laid-back person ever.

"You all right?"

I blush and duck my head. "I kind of met someone. It's a long story."

"Tell me later. The guys we hired for tonight are getting restless."

I hurry to the stage and say a quick hello to the drummer. I'm not sure where the other guy is but I'm too flustered to do anything more than check my equipment. I'm not surprised to find that Trent has everything ready for me. "Thank you."

"No problem." He picks up his guitar and lifts his chin.

The bassist, a guy I don't recognize, throws a scowl at me as he struts onto the stage.

I don't need to look at the list. I know it by heart. All the same cover songs you'd expect to hear in a place like the Tipsy Saddle. There's also a short list of my own songs. I'm pretty sure the bass player rolls his eyes at one point but I pay him no mind. It's not the first time I've been dismissed and it certainly won't be the last. No one's paying him to perform *his* original material tonight, so he can suck it.

When we're finished rehearsing our set, Trent walks the guys to the back door. Once they're out of sight, I pull out my acoustic guitar and drop down onto a bench.

Soft boot steps over the hardwood stop my strumming. "Something new you want to work on?" Trent asks, watching me carefully.

"A few lyrics have been floating around in my head all morning." Even though we've spent many hours writing together, this feels too personal to share details.

"Break-up song?"

"Hardly." No, it wasn't Brad on my mind this morning. Not even after the ugly scene at my house. Rooster is the only man occupying my thoughts.

I strum a few chords and allow the words to flow out.

Trent raises an eyebrow and chuckles. "Must be some story."

He helps me work out the melody on the old backstage piano. It still needs finessing, but I like where it's headed.

After rehearsal, my manager stops by to discuss tour plans. I still can't believe I have an actual manager. But Greg's been such a help to me over the last month.

For the rest of the day, I help get the bar ready to open.

In the free hour I have before I have to go on stage, my mother stops by with my dress.

I can't help bouncing up and down on my toes when I see it. "It's so pretty."

"Finished it this morning."

I hold it up against my chest and swish the layered skirt back and forth. It's white chiffon with teal flowers and a skirt meant for twirling. I probably have fifty other ones just like it in my closet, but this is my favorite style. Under the stage lights, I tend to sweat through a lot of dresses. Thank the Lord, my mom can sew.

"It's perfect." I lean in to kiss her cheek. "Thank you."

She hands me a small brown paper bag. I peek inside and grin. Little matching teal booty shorts to thwart the pervy guys who always try to take upskirt shots. "Thanks, Mom."

"So, I'm guessing you had a sleepover?" she raises one eyebrow.

"What makes you say that?"

Her stern-mom eyes drill holes in me. "The condom wrappers in your room."

"Mom! Jesus." I crush the dress and paper bag to my chest and dart a quick look around the room. Sandra's busy stacking clean glasses. One of our regulars is staring at the muted television screen over the bar. Neither of them so much as glance our way. "Really?" My harsh whisper has an edgy whine to it.

She snickers and sips her drink. "I hope it was Rooster and not Brad."

"Yes, it was Rooster. Brad and I are *done*."

"Good. That boy was all hat and no cattle."

I snort at her description of Brad.

"Rooster looks like he's *all* cattle," she adds.

"Why are you so happy about me having a fling with a guy who's leaving town in a couple of weeks?"

"Because now isn't the time for you to be tied down. You've got a big tour and all sorts of opportunities opening up. But that doesn't mean you shouldn't have some fun." Her smile fades. "Just be careful. Guard your heart carefully, Shelby. And don't get yourself into *trouble* like I did."

Sure, my mom's own dreams of stardom were shattered when she got pregnant with me. My whole life she's drummed it into my head to avoid getting pregnant at all costs. Hell, she even gave me a box of condoms on my fifteenth birthday.

I understand her concern, even if the reminder that I ruined her life stings.

"Is he going to come watch you tonight?" she asks.

"No, I didn't even tell him."

"What? Why not?"

I shrug, not sure I can put it into words. It was nice being with someone who didn't know anything about the last year of my life. Clearly, Rooster didn't consume a lot of reality television. Just the kind of person I need in my life right now.

"Like you said." I swallow hard and can't quite meet her eyes. "I don't want to be tied down."

Truth is, I can't afford a broken heart right now.

CHAPTER THIRTEEN

Rooster

THE DOUBLE SHOT OF TEQUILA CURRENTLY BURNING ITS WAY down my throat is damn good. It had been served to me between two giant tits. The bartender seemed to serve everyone that way, so I wasn't special. Although, she'd made it clear she'd be more than willing to sneak in the back and suck me off if I wanted.

Normally, I'd be jamming my cock down her throat a few minutes after that type of offer. Tonight, the only woman on my mind is one particular tiny blonde. One I've been searching for ever since we arrived. Maybe I got the name wrong. Shelby can't possibly work in this dump.

Murphy and his old lady, Heidi, tagged along tonight. Doubt they'll stay long, but I appreciate their company. Heidi's a smart, thoughtful old lady. Grew up around the club since her brother's the treasurer of our upstate charter. Loyal as fuck to the club, even though she's barely twenty-one. Can't blame Murphy one bit for claiming her ass as soon as he could.

Jigsaw, Ravage, and Sparky also rode with us. They're busy prowling the bar in search of non-clubwhore pussy.

Soft fingers brush the back of my hand. "Sure you're not interested in something sweeter?" The bartender's southern drawl comes out harsh and grating. Nothing like the sweet honey that passes Shelby's lips.

"No," I grunt at her. Christ, I should've turned Jiggy loose on this chick. She sure can't seem to grasp that *I'm* not interested.

Finally, she turns her predatory gaze on Murphy who doesn't even notice the target on his big, ginger head. The laser-focused stink-eye Heidi shoots the flirty bartender makes me chuckle into my beer. No one messes with Heidi's man.

The bartender sends Heidi a wink and nod before finally moving along to her next...customer.

Now, where the hell is Shelby?

The lights blink a few times. As if it's some sort of signal and not a sign of failing electric, people move away from the bar. Curious, I turn just as the room is plunged into darkness.

Cheesy blue and white lights sweep the room, finally landing in the corner.

Murphy elbows me. "Guess they actually use that stage."

When we'd made our way down the rickety wooden staircase into this little honky-tonk paradise, we'd passed several signs declaring there'd be "live music" tonight. Heidi had shown more interest in it than any of us. It'll probably be some hillbilly country crap that will make me want to stab a steak knife in my ears.

With the barest amount of interest, I glance at the stage. Irritation that I still haven't seen Shelby colors my mood even blacker than normal.

A spotlight shines down, bathing the slightly elevated wooden platform with golden light. Four figures saunter out and fiddle with instruments.

A few seconds later someone to my right gasps. People murmur and strain to see the stage. Cheers go up and a large portion of the crowd rushes forward. Over the small sea of jostling bodies, familiar blonde curls bounce into view.

Is that...Shelby?

"How y'all doing tonight!?" she shouts at the crowd, raising her hand in the air.

I sit up and crane my neck to get a better look. She's wearing an innocent enough flowered dress with well-worn, brown leather cowboy boots covered in long fringe. Underneath the pounds of makeup and big hair, I recognize my Shelby.

"Oh!" Heidi bounces up and down. "The sign outside

said one of the winners of *Redneck Roadhouse Star* is performing live tonight. That must be her."

I turn and stare at her. "Redneck *what*?"

She shrugs. "Some reality country music star finding show. Trinity and I watched it a bunch of times. Even got Hope to watch it with us once or twice."

Shelby's some kind of reality television star? A singer?

Reality television, hell television in general, isn't something I waste my time with. If she's so famous, why's she slinging cinnamon rolls at that cheap diner?

The music starts up. Same kind of twangy shit that's been assaulting my ears since my club invaded Texas. Not that country music isn't popular in New York, but down here, it seems to be a religion.

Then Shelby opens her mouth and the voice of an angel floats out. Corny as fuck? Maybe. I don't exactly know how else to describe what I'm hearing.

All her shyness seems to evaporate onstage. She vibrates with the bold sass I've witnessed a few times. Big voice, big personality. Fucking beautiful.

Most days, I'd rather shoot myself than listen to country music, but I could listen to Shelby caress that microphone all damn night.

Why didn't she tell me?

Because you're just a fuck.

I know I'd made it clear I wasn't sticking around for long, but I thought we connected enough for her to tell me she's kind of a big deal.

Christ, it's been what, forty-eight hours, and I've turned into a whiny pussy over this chick? My motto has always been love 'em and leave 'em smiling. So, I should be thrilled she's only interested in me as a dick to ride and nothing more, right?

During one part of the performance, the guitarist rubs up on her. They share an intimate look while singing a duet. Maybe it's all an act, but the dude seems to be in love with her. Is it for the crowd? Are they involved? Will Blaise be pissed if I bury a body on his club's property tonight?

Does it matter if these two fuck on the regular? Is it my business? Maybe not, but the idea sure annoys the shit out of me.

The place fills up with more and more people. Doesn't seem to be any sort of security keeping things in check. I scan the door every few minutes in case Brad decides to show his face. I'm sure that joker knows all about Shelby's musical talents.

Jigsaw leans up against me and slaps my back. "Isn't that your girl?"

"Yup."

"You didn't tell us she was famous."

"I didn't know," I grumble.

"She's good."

"Yeah," I agree, without taking my eyes off her.

Shelby fascinates me on several different levels. I've never met a woman quite like her.

The band goes through several more songs before the

lights go out again. People crowd the edge of the stage, waiting for Shelby to sign stuff or take photos with them. I sit back and watch as she interacts with the crowd. Her *fans*, I guess.

Damn. It shouldn't surprise me, but she's sweet and patient with everyone who waves a napkin to sign in her face.

Finally, she's free, and she heads straight for the bar. As soon as she sees me, she slows her steps. Her eyes widen. Her jaw drops.

"Rooster? What're you doing here?" The hesitation vanishes, and she grins wide, running over and flinging her arms around my neck. I catch her and lean down to kiss her bright red lips.

"You're something else." I press my forehead to hers and lower my voice. "Why didn't you say something?"

She shrugs and signals the bartender to bring her some water.

"Shelby?" I prod.

"Can we talk about it later? I have another set." She swoops in and kisses my cheek. "I'm real happy to see ya, though."

I introduce her to Heidi and Murphy.

Shelby turns to me and rakes her nails through my hair a few times. I fight the urge to close my eyes and lean into her touch. "If your hair were a few shades red, you and Murphy could be brothers."

I flick my gaze at Murphy and smirk. "Well, no one's ever said *that* before."

"I'm insulted." Murphy laughs and strokes his fingers over his beard. "But I'll let it slide since my girl's such a big fan of yours."

Heidi grins and smacks Murphy's shoulder.

"Sparky and Ravage are around here somewhere." I point to Jigsaw as he prowls up to us. "You remember this clown."

She wiggles her fingers at him. "Hi, Jigsaw."

Heidi gushes over Shelby's performance, and the two of them start speed-talking about music. Murphy glances at me and lifts his shoulders.

While she's invested in her conversation with Heidi, Shelby's butt rests against my thigh, her fingers laced with mine. Like the pervy fucker I am, I spend some time enjoying the view down the front of her dress.

The guitar player cowboys his way over, stopping and throwing a dark scowl at Shelby when he notices her ass in my lap.

"Shelby? Who are your friends?" he asks, without acknowledging me.

Murphy's mouth twists in an *are-we-killing-this-disrespectful-punk* sort of way. I give him a subtle head shake. Not yet.

"Oh! Trent. This is my friend, Rooster."

Friend. Huh.

I'm busy mulling over how I feel about *friend* while she

introduces Murphy and Heidi. When there's a lull in the conversation, I squeeze her hip and brush my lips against her ear. "I think I'm a lil' more than your friend, Sugar."

She leans back and gives me a sultry look before whispering in my ear. "Did you want me to introduce you as my fuck-buddy?"

"No," I growl.

She pulls back and turns to stare at me.

"Never mind." I flash a smile at her. "I'm just messing with you. You're a pretty damn good singer." Fuck, that's inadequate.

"Thanks. It's been a crazy year." Her cheeks turn pink, and she lowers her lashes. "I play some of my own, original stuff during the next set if you want to stick around."

Of course I'm staying. "None of that was yours?"

"No, silly." She scrunches up her nose. "You don't listen to country, do you?"

"Not if I can help it."

Not insulted, she laughs and slaps my chest.

Fuck, I want her under me again tonight.

CHAPTER FOURTEEN

Shelby

DANG. ROOSTER HAS ME RATTLED RIGHT DOWN TO MY LUCKY boots.

Never in a million years did I expect him to remember what the cops said and come find me here tonight.

The sexy, confident way he was leaning back on the bar with both elbows, facing me, left me breathless. Then it sunk in, he came here to see *me*. Specifically, for me. He didn't drop in to a random bar for a drink and run into me accidentally. He wanted to see me again.

I end up rubbing against him like a horny little kitten, wondering if it will be totally detrimental to my career if I take him in the storage room and...

"Shelby, let's go!" Trent shouts.

"Are you staying?" I ask Rooster.

"Wouldn't miss it."

He gives me a quick kiss for luck and a gentle shove into the crowd.

Knowing he's out there watching—with his friends no less—leaves me jittery. Trent nudges my arm as I step on stage.

"You okay?" he mouths.

"I'm fine."

"We still tryin' out that new song?"

"Maybe. Let's see how the crowd reacts." Lord, I'm a wuss tonight.

He throws a scowl in Rooster's direction. "That your new boyfriend?"

"Sort of." Now I wish like hell I'd never worked on the new song with Trent this morning. He's smart enough to add up two plus two and come up with Rooster as the inspiration for my song.

Trent grunts and turns around, giving me his back.

Forget him. Rooster's out in the crowd. Listening to me sing. Every word. Watching me. I don't think I can go through with playing the new song now. No way.

The lights go down, and the band kicks in. I close my eyes and absorb the thump and twang of the music. After a few beats, all my worries and insecurities float away on the warm wind blowing over the stage, courtesy of two giant metal fans.

It's just me and the music now. Where I'm happiest. Doesn't matter that it's a dumpy little bar in Texas. Or a huge stage in front of a television audience. Even as a little girl, music touched me emotionally in a way simple words never could. The throb of the music lights me up inside, and I thrive on sharing beautiful words with the strangers filling the bar.

As silly as it might sound to some people, *Redneck Roadhouse Star* had been my dream come true. My chance to be seen as more than the poor girl in the handmade dresses who won every talent competition in Bexar county. The show also opened my eyes to what the music business was really about. I was nothing more than a minnow swimming with sharks. It left me cynical. But I poured my disappointment into my music, giving it a grown-up jaded quality it lacked before.

Every cloud has a rhinestone-studded lining, right?

Sure, online gossip sites were full of people mocking me. Everyone seemed to think my blonde curls and big boobs indicated I was dimmer than a dying light bulb. People commented and criticized my weight so many times I still can't eat food in public for fear of an unflattering photo showing up somewhere.

All the scrutiny eased up a little once I came home. I hadn't made it to the end of the show or won the big prize, but I'd gotten enough attention to win an opening spot on a major tour. I planned to make the best of it. Ride it out as long as I can and pray like hell I make it to the top.

People 'round here seemed to assume being on television equaled rolling in money. But the show barely replaced the wages I lost from leaving my job for so long. I won't make any money until I start touring, and even then, from what I understood of the contract I signed, I'll be making pennies.

"Let's do it." Trent hands me a guitar and nods. "You've got this, Shelby. It's good. Real damn good."

Even though I sensed his annoyance earlier, Trent's always encouraging and supportive where music's concerned.

Music has always given me a way to express the things I shouldn't say but couldn't keep quiet about. But tonight, my hands shake at the thought of speaking a little too much truth to this audience. None of my other songs are this personal. And no one I've ever written a song about has watched me perform it in such an intimate setting.

Trent stops the band and takes the microphone, something he rarely does. "Miss Shelby has something brand new she wants to play for y'all tonight. She's a lil' nervous, though, so how 'bout some encouragement!"

"Show us your tits!" someone screams.

"That ain't what I meant." Trent scowls into the crowd, searching for the degenerate who's mistaken the Tipsy Saddle for a strip club.

I turn on my southern charm and flash a megawatt smile at the crowd. "Well, this song definitely ain't about *that* guy."

"I love you, Shelby!" someone else shouts.

My laughter comes out husky and soft through the microphone. "Thank you."

I strum my fingers over the strings. Out of the corner of my eye, I catch Trent's nod.

My mouth opens, but no sound comes out.

Fear rolls over me. When Trent and I went over the song earlier, I never imagined singing it in front of Rooster.

It shouldn't be such a big deal. With all the bright lights shining in my eyes, I can't actually *see* Rooster's face. I assume he's still over by the bar.

Besides, it's so loud. The sound system isn't great. The crowd's boisterous. He probably won't be able to understand the words anyway.

Or maybe the song will scare him away before I finish my set. Then my heart won't have to endure the utter humiliation of watching him run out the door in horror.

I take a deep breath and close my eyes.

"*Sometimes your white knight rides a Harley*
　　And he doesn't need an army
　　To save you from drowning
　　In three feet of water..."

CHAPTER FIFTEEN

Rooster

WITH ALL THE NOISE AND THE SHITTY SPEAKERS, IT'S BEEN harder than hell to make out any of the words Shelby's sung tonight.

Something about this new song she's singing, though, has me pushing through the crowd to get closer.

I definitely pick out the word *Harley* and close my eyes to concentrate on the rest.

SOON I'LL BE SINGING *in a different town.*
    And you'll give some other girl your crown.

REPLACE CROWN with *cock* and I'm pretty sure she's singing

about *us*. Did I really inspire her that much? Or am I reading more into it? Have I lost my motherfucking mind?

Jigsaw slaps my shoulder. "Are you sleeping through her song?"

"No, asshole," I growl, annoyed I missed a couple of words.

He jerks his chin toward the stage. "She's so fucking hot. I get why you're torqued up over her, brother."

"Thanks. I've been dying for your approval."

Shelby starts in on the chorus again, and I elbow Jigsaw. "Shut up."

"*SOMETIMES YOUR WHITE knight rides a Harley*
He doesn't need an army
To save you from drowning
In three feet of water..."

"HOLY FUCK!" Jigsaw doubles over laughing. "That's *you*. She wrote a song about you." He straightens up and pretends to be serious. "I'll cover you if you want to make a run for it."

"Fuck off. I'm not going anywhere."

"*I KNEW I was in danger*
Of losing my heart to a stranger."

· · ·

Maybe I'm more than just a fuck after all.

Jigsaw's too annoying to concentrate on the song any longer. The audience is getting rowdier, too. We sway with every push and two-step of the crowd.

Shelby finishes our song with her eyes closed and a smile on her face. Can't help but notice her expression is similar to how she looks after I make her come.

Now I can't stop thinking about her sweet naked body.

The band kicks into a livelier song that makes the crowd holler and move even faster. Who knew country fans were so excitable? We're packed in like sardines, so I go along for the ride.

How does Shelby do this every week? Does she play other local bars? I glance around the bar. Still seems to be no security or anyone watching over the place. Who protects her from these idiots if they get out of hand?

Her guitarist rattles off the name of another song, but I'm too focused on a group of guys clustered to the side of the stage who seem to be ducking and laughing every time Shelby turns away from them.

"What the fuck are they up to?" I slap Jigsaw to get his attention off the brunette in front of us whose tits are two hoedown throwdown steps away from jiggling out of her top.

"Huh? Who?"

"The bros up front." I grab his head and turn it to the left.

He stares at them for a few seconds before unleashing a vicious growl. "Assholes." He shakes me off and pushes harder through the crowd.

"What?"

"Pretty sure they're trying to take some upskirt photos of your girl," he answers, without taking his eyes off his future punching bags.

Jiggy may be a perverted asshole ninety-five percent of the time, but even he has lines that shouldn't be crossed.

I watch the guys closer, taking in Shelby's guarded expression and the way she's now avoiding that side of the stage.

Jigsaw better step aside. I'm about to fuck up some assholes for trying to take advantage of my girl.

CHAPTER SIXTEEN

Shelby

SWEAT'S POURING DOWN MY FACE BY THE TIME WE FINISH
Big Lies—my favorite of the new songs I'd written while
on Redneck Roadhouse. Thank the Lord for stage
makeup. I survived playing White Knight by keeping my
gaze far away from Rooster's side of the bar. The couple
songs we played afterward took my anxiety away, but now,
it returns with a vengeance.

What if Rooster left?

"Good job!" Trent shouts as the lights fade. He high-
fives the rest of the band.

"Tonight was a good one, right?" I laugh and hug him,
allowing him to pick me up for a quick spin around the
stage.

He sets me down and kisses my cheek. "Gonna make sure the guys get paid." He glances at the crowd. "You okay out here?"

"I'll be fine. Go on." I pat his shoulder. "Thank you."

As soon as the guys leave, people rush and push to get closer to me. I don't know if it's the radio coverage the show was given or something else, but the simple barrier the club uses to keep some space between the floor and the stage isn't strong enough to keep the audience back tonight.

My blood spikes with fear. More than the anxiety of Rooster hearing my song. My gaze darts toward the bar, but I don't see him. Still blinded from the show, I can't see much besides darkness, dots of light and a hoard of people coming for me.

"Shelby! I love you!" A kid close to my age shouts. He shoves something in my face, and I back away so quickly, I trip, landing hard on my ass. My dress pools around my hips. Booty shorts or not, I hurry to push it down and cover myself.

Maybe they don't see me sprawled on the floor or maybe they don't care, but the crowd keeps coming, A sea of boots and jeans threaten to drown me. Or stomp me to death.

I search for anything to grab onto, trying to right myself, but keep getting knocked right back down.

The guy who'd startled me bends down, hand

outstretched. But, instead of attempting to help me, he runs his hands up my bare legs and under my dress.

I shudder with revulsion at the unwanted grope.

"Get off me!" I pull my legs back and launch both my snip-toe cowboy booted feet forward as hard as I can, hitting him square in his chest—heels first. "Fucker."

He reels back, then rights himself and lunges again. I desperately search for something to whack him with. My mic stand's just out of reach.

Suddenly, the crowd parts. The guy who touched me sails through the air, crashing into a nearby table. Wood clatters to the floor and glass shatters against the wall.

"Motherfucker!"

I recognize that rage-filled, growly voice.

"Rooster!" I yelp.

Fury twists his features when he spots me on the floor. He easily bends down and plucks me off the ground. "You okay?"

"I'm fine." I wrap my arms around his neck and cling to him. Now that I know I'm safe, the fear and indignation evaporates but leaves my entire body shaking.

And I have no doubt I'm safe. Murphy and Jigsaw are busy throwing punches at the frat boys who kept trying to take pictures up my dress during the show. Sparky and another biker wearing the same patches as Rooster are shoving people out of our way.

Heidi's sitting cross-legged on top of the bar, holding

what I'm pretty sure is a ballpeen hammer in her hands. She grins when she sees me but stays put. Rooster sets me on the bar next to her.

"You all right?" he shouts.

"Yeah." My mouth twists. "Shit. My mic is on stage. It's actually mine. Not the bar's. It cost me a fortune."

"I'll get it." His gaze swings to Heidi. "Stay with Heidi."

"Okay." I tug on his hand before he returns to the mayhem of the crowded bar. "Thank you."

"You got it. Stay here," he reminds me.

Heidi wraps an arm around my shoulders. "You're amazing! Your voice is beautiful." She reaches behind her and hands me a bottle of water. "Bet you're parched."

"Yeah." I take a long swallow before capping it and setting it next to me.

"Girl, this is wild," Heidi says. "Does this happen every night?"

"Not this bad." I glance at the hammer in her hands. "Planning to do some remodeling?"

She gives me a sly grin. "Murphy set me on the bar, gave me the hammer, and told me to stay put. Anyone who bothers me is getting bopped on the head." She taps the air with the hammer to demonstrate.

"Aren't you tougher than a pine knot," I mutter, impressed that none of this seems to ruffle her feathers. And that her boyfriend apparently doesn't leave home without a hammer to use as a weapon in case they encounter a little mayhem.

"He wanted to stay with me." Heidi waves her hands at the stage. "But I'm fine. Looked like you needed the help."

"Yeah." I glance around for our bartender, Sherry, but she's nowhere to be found. "Shit, Sherry's probably calling the cops."

As the word *cops* leaves my lips, Heidi gracefully stands on top of the bar and whistles an ear-splitting sound to get Murphy's attention. She makes a few hand signals that must be code for "Police are on the way!" Murphy taps Jigsaw's shoulder and says a few words against his ear. Jigsaw whistles and signals to the others. A few seconds later, all five bikers slowly back out of the chaos and return to us at the bar.

Sherry reappears.

With a shotgun in her hands.

She aims at the ceiling and fires. A deafening blast that puts an abrupt end to the fighting. Chunks of wood spray down over the center of the bar.

Rooster slips his arm around me. "Where was she ten minutes ago?" he mutters.

I can't help it. Maybe it's the fear or adrenaline, but I press my palms against his face and yank him down for a kiss.

"Thank you," I whisper against his lips.

"Thank me later when I get you out of here before the cops show up." He pulls back a few inches. "You're trouble, little darlin'."

He's teasing, but I melt against him anyway. In his arms, I know I'm safe.

He eyes Sherry who's still holding the shotgun. "I think she's got it under control." He turns to his brothers. "Let's go."

CHAPTER SEVENTEEN

Rooster

ANOTHER NIGHT AND I FIND MYSELF ON AN EXCRUCIATING ride back to Shelby's place. Maybe I should just start paying her mom rent.

Except, tonight I'm not planning to stay long. She's coming with me. After that shitshow at the Tipsy Saddle, I won't let her wander far from my sight. In fact, I follow her right into her bedroom.

"Are you hungry?" I ask.

"I can never eat after a show, I'm still too jittery and wound up."

Makes sense.

"So." My lips twitch as I draw out the word. "I've never been accused of being someone's White Knight before."

Shelby stops and turns, wide eyes blinking. A sweet

shade of red spreads over her cheeks and down her chest. "What?"

"Your song."

She lowers her gaze. "I was hoping you couldn't make out the words."

"Why? I'm more worried you'll tell people it's about me, and they won't believe it."

"Are you kidding?" She steps closer. "You may come in denim and leather instead of shining armor, but you've rescued me twice now. Three times if you count chasing Brad away from my door this morning."

"Saw that kick you landed on that one fool's chest." I push her hair back off her cheek. "So, I'm not sure you needed the rescue, but I'm damn glad I was there."

"Me too."

My hand drops to her shoulder, and I skim the strap of her dress with my fingers. "This is pretty."

"My mama made it."

Somehow that doesn't surprise me. It fits Shelby's curves and personality.

She twists her fingers in the fabric swirling around her legs. "There's a secret to it."

"To what?" I'm too focused on the bits of bare leg she's revealing as she lifts the material.

"Matching shorts." She flips the skirt up, revealing a pair of tight little shorts the same shade of blue-green as the flowers scattered all over the dress.

I run my hand over my beard as I take her in.

"Jackasses trying to take pictures up my dress is nothing new," she explains.

Instantly, my lust flips to rage. "Those motherfuckers. I didn't punch them nearly enough."

"You punched them?"

"Fuck yeah, I did. The ones I didn't get, Jiggy handled."

"I'm sorry your brothers had to get involved in my mess."

"They've always got my back. No matter what."

She reaches for my hands, turning them over to inspect my scraped knuckles. "You should let me put ice on 'em."

"I had something more healing in mind."

"Like what?" Her question comes out coy.

I brush my bruised knuckles over her shoulder. "Like soft skin and that honey voice of yours."

"Honey, huh?"

"Smooth and sweet."

"You're smooth and sweet."

I clutch my chest and throw my head back. "You're killing me, woman."

She turns and sweeps her hair into a ponytail. "Will you unzip my dress?"

"With pleasure." As if I'd say no to undressing this beautiful woman. My fingers graze the zipper, and I pause, inspired by a better idea. "Place your hands on the bed." The way she doesn't hesitate or question me does wonders for my already enormous ego.

I step closer and trail my fingers over the backs of her thighs, lifting her dress as I go, uncovering the surprise underneath. "These are cute."

Instead of answering, she wiggles her butt.

"Want me to take them off?"

"If you want to," she whispers.

I smack her ass hard enough to make her gasp. "What do *you* want?"

Her body tightens up against me. I slide my hand between her thighs, exploring the damp satin material clinging to her pussy. "You're soaked."

"I'm all sweaty."

"I don't think that's sweat."

"Oh!" she gasps, as I slide my fingers over her clit.

Even with the thin material in the way, I keep my touch light. Slowly stroking until her hips move in time with me. "That's it," I encourage.

"Rooster," she whispers.

Before answering, I hook my fingers in her underwear and drag them down her legs, stopping along the way to kiss the small of her back, each butt cheek and the backs of her thighs.

"You're so damn pretty." I kiss her soft skin in between words. "The way you worked that stage was something else." Having her bent over in front of me has my dick ready to tear through my jeans.

She snorts into the sheets. "It's nothing but a little bar."

I smack her ass again. "Doesn't matter. Any fool can see you're destined for bigger things."

This time, she has no sassy comeback. She's too busy moaning and panting as I slide my fingers up her thigh and through the soft, wet flesh between her legs. The ferocious need to be inside her practically blinds me.

CHAPTER EIGHTEEN

Shelby

My mind's gone. I'm usually wound up after a show and can't sit still, but with Rooster's fingers sliding back and forth between my legs, I'm practically melting into my mattress.

"Please don't stop."

"I have no intention of stopping."

I love the gruff but reassuring tone he uses with me. His fingers haven't stopped moving, the heat he's creating down there continues to build. Air bursts past my lips as he slips one finger all the way inside, curling and stroking until my body clenches tight. Molten-hot pleasure shoots through me. My heart beats hummingbird fast. I don't think I've ever been so turned on. How is he still so calm and in control?

My toes curl in my boots, and I squeeze my eyes shut, desperately trying to leap onto the freight train of pleasure barreling down on me. Heat races over my skin.

"Will you come for me, Shelby?" His whispered question holds a note of teasing. "Come all over my hand for me."

The pressure inside me breaks as I finally let go. Quivering heat crashes through me, leaving me breathless and my legs shaking so hard I can barely stand. He slips his fingers out of me but stays pressed against my body.

There's a crinkling sound. His body shifts. The rough fabric of his jeans tickles my legs. A few seconds later, he drags his cock along my slit. "Think you can take more?" he teases.

"God, yes. Please." I don't even care how desperate and eager I sound.

He withdraws completely, cool air replacing his warmth over my bare skin. His body brushes my side as he flops down on the bed in front of me. "Come ride me."

"Beard or cock?"

Laughter dances in his eyes. He strokes his hand up and down his cock, showing off. "Lady's choice."

I strip off my dress and bra, but when I bend over to take off my boots, Rooster sits up and stops me. "Leave the boots on."

He grips my hip and guides me into the bed. I throw my leg over him, straddling his hips.

"Damn, I'm a lucky bastard," he whispers. "Every man in that bar would've killed to go home with you."

"Well, you're the only man I wanted to take home." I rock back and forth, teasing him for a second before stopping. "I don't take guys home with me from the bar. Or anywhere, usually. You're—" I don't know why I feel the sudden urge to explain myself.

He sits up, pressing his palms against my cheeks. "Wouldn't matter to me if you did."

That's not exactly reassuring for some reason.

"Life's too short for games or regret." His low, rumbling voice hints at a deeper meaning. He brushes a soft kiss over my lips, beard tickling my skin. "You my girl tonight?"

I glance down but can't escape his hold or his smoldering gaze. "Yes."

"Good. Now, choose a ride."

Finding a handful of courage, I wrap my hand around his cock. "This is lookin' mighty fine."

He chuckles and moves closer to kiss my cheek, down to my neck. His hands move from my face to tangle in my hair, holding me still, while our lips meet and our tongues twine together. My nipples harden to throbbing points. He breaks our kiss and dips down to devour my breasts with hot, wet kisses and licks.

Another explosion simmers deep inside me. "Logan."

His lips return to mine, swallowing my plea. His hands drop to my hips, urging me up.

Excited energy burns through me, and I grip his cock again, slowly stroking up and down. "Gosh, I'm not sure this will fit."

He growls and nips my earlobe. "You already know we fit together perfectly."

Perfectly.

Nothing in my whole life has ever been perfect.

Except the few moments I've spent with Rooster this week.

That's a dangerous road to go down, Shelby.

I rise up on my knees and center myself over him. He stares up at me, eyes glowing with anticipation.

Inch by inch, I take him inside me, awed at how amazing he feels. The satisfied groan he lets out triggers me to move faster.

"Ah, fuck." He squeezes his eyes shut and bucks his hips.

I lean down and press kisses over his chest. He answers by gripping my hair and tugging me up. "Ride. Me."

"Like this?" I tease, twitching my hips. Desperate for something to hold onto, I take his hands. I lift and rock myself up and down his shaft. Each movement is a shock of electricity to my system.

"Harder," he demands, watching me intently.

His hands move to my breasts, cupping and flicking his thumbs over my nipples. The raw appreciation on his face erases any embarrassment I might have had about the way they bounce and sway.

My cheap metal bed frame squeaks and thumps into the wall. Thank God my mother's not home. I work myself up and down his length even harder, searching for the spot that will set me off.

The orgasm hits me hard and fast, exploding through my body in a pounding rush. Rooster barely lets me ride it out before flipping us. The weight of him comforts and crushes me. He pounds into me with wicked thrusts. I scrabble to grab and hold onto his ass, digging my nails into the muscle.

His pace slows and turns erratic as he groans through his release. Finally, he opens his eyes and smiles down at me. "I hope you're not too tired. We definitely need to do that again."

All the events of the day come rushing back. Any exhaustion I should be feeling is held back by orgasmic bliss.

Something tugs at the corner of my eye and I realize I never took off my stage makeup. I slap my hands over my face. "Oh, hell. I must be a mess."

Rooster's beard tickles my fingers as he brushes a kiss over my knuckles. "A hot, freshly fucked mess."

I squint through my fingers at him, afraid to move my hands because I'm pretty sure one of my false eyelashes is loose. "Thanks. I think."

He rolls to the side and stands. "I'll be right back."

I follow him to the bathroom. Leaning over the sink, I scrub my face clean.

"Now you're even prettier." Rooster gathers my hair into a ponytail and kisses my shoulder.

Sweet Lord.

How is it that every time he opens his mouth, he makes it harder and harder to protect my heart?

CHAPTER NINETEEN

Rooster

"I hate to sound like a bad cliché, but I don't suppose you have any denim cut-offs?" I lean back on my elbows, watching as Shelby stuffs clothes into a small backpack. So far I've counted five pairs of socks. Not sure where she thinks I'm taking her that requires so much foot protection, but it's cute.

Still gloriously naked, except for her cowboy boots, she smiles over her shoulder. "What good southern gal doesn't have a pair of Daisy Dukes in her wardrobe?"

She opens a drawer and shakes out a pair of faded denim, frayed at the edges. "My cheeks don't hang out of 'em, but it's the best I've got."

"Those'll work. No one needs to see your sweet ass but me."

She raises an eyebrow but doesn't comment on my caveman opinion.

"What's your favorite color?" Shit, did I really just ask her that? Is her pussy so fucking magical that it has the power to turn me back into a teenager?

She stops rolling the T-shirt in her hands and stares at me. "My favorite color?" Each word comes out slowly, as if no one's asked her such a basic question since she was in first grade.

I shrug. "I already know you come like a rocket when you're on top." In fact, my dick's getting hard again just thinking about it. "Figured I should learn some other things."

"Electric teal."

Slowly, I sit up and repeat the words back to her. "That's specific."

"Teal, mint green, baby blue. Girly colors without being *pink*." She makes a face as if pink is the most horrible color she can imagine.

That suits her.

She bends down and pulls off one boot and then the other.

"Damn, it was hot as fuck watching you prance around with the boots and nothing else."

One corner of her mouth slides up. "I've got a nice black pair I was planning to bring with me."

Thank fuck I have my own room at the ranch.

She finishes packing then slips on a pair of jeans, a T-shirt, and a beat-up leather jacket that's seen better days. "Ready." She reaches into her closet and scoops up a pair of black, cowboy boots. "Can't forget these."

"Nope."

We're almost to the front door when she stops and hurries back to the kitchen. "Wait, I need to leave my mom a note, or she'll worry." The concern in Shelby's tone reaches right into my chest and squeezes my heart.

"You two are tight."

"Have to be. We only got each other." She shuffles through some papers on the counter until she finds a notepad. "Been that way for a long time."

She doesn't say it in a sad way or a pity me way. It's just a fact for Shelby.

When she finishes scribbling down a few words, I motion for her to hand me the pad, so I can leave my own message.

Lynn-

If you need anything, call me. 518-555-0907.

Logan Randall (Rooster)

After scanning my note, Shelby's jaw drops. She stares up at me. "Thank you. That was...well, thank you."

"I don't want her to worry." I give her a sly smile to lighten things up. "Jigsaw extended an invite to her if you think she'll be interested."

"That's a *hell no*." She slaps our note on the counter and shoves me toward the door.

"What? Your mom seems like she knows how to party."

She groans. "I'm sure she does. I don't want to witness it, though."

"Maybe she could finally turn Jiggy into a man."

"My mama's got no patience for boys."

"Yeah, exactly."

Outside, she chuckles when I hand her a brand-new helmet. Her laughter abruptly stops as she stares at the headgear. "Did you borrow this from someone?"

"Worried about lice?"

"What?" She scrunches her nose. "No."

"Stopped at a shop and bought it for you. Figured it'll come in handy while I'm down here."

She's quiet and her expression has me realizing that might have come off kind of presumptuous. She didn't expect me to come to the bar tonight to see her play. Yet, here I am, prepared to take her back to my place helmet and all. Poor girl's probably starting to wonder if I got a basement with a pit and a bottle of lotion waiting for her.

"It's not a ring, Shelby."

"Huh?" She meets my eyes again. "Oh. It's not that. I... appreciate it. That was real sweet of you, Logan."

"You keep accusing me of being sweet, I'm going to develop a complex."

She tilts her head to the side. "What's the matter? The other big bad bikers won't let you play with 'em if they find out you got a sweet side?"

Damn, I love how that southern accent gets even twangier when she's throwing sass at me.

CHAPTER TWENTY

Shelby

My poor, pitiful heart's in real trouble.

Orgasms by the bucketload—*check.*

Thoughtful enough to leave his number for my mom —*check.*

Fills out a pair of jeans nicely—*double check.*

If I were looking for a man, Rooster ticks all my boxes.

Except for that whole living in New York thing.

And that I'm on the verge of finally having my dream career.

Let's not forget, that except for his manners and bedroom skills, I don't know a whole lot about him.

"So where are you taking me again?"

"The ranch I'm staying at. It's a friend's place. Couple of other clubs are there, so stick with me."

"Will Heidi be there?"

His lips curl up. "Yeah, she'll be there. Her brother and his girl should be there, too. You and Heidi seemed to hit it off. That's good."

Why does that seem important to him? "She was something with that hammer and then whistling to you guys when I warned her the cops might show up."

"Yeah, she's a loyal old lady."

I raise an eyebrow. "I think she's younger than me."

"It's...never mind." He hesitates, which is odd, since Rooster doesn't seem to be one to mince words. "Murphy's itching to put a weddin' band on her finger as soon as she's done with school."

From his expression, it's impossible to tell if Rooster wants the same for himself or if he's just amused by his friend. "She mentioned they're gettin' married this summer."

He nods, opens his mouth, shakes his head, then smiles at me. "Yeah, it'll be a big event. Whole club will be there."

Was he considering asking me to...be his date? Or am I reading too much into it his behavior?

He nods to his Harley, ending my speculation. After helping me strap on the new helmet, he straddles the bike and motions for me to get on behind him.

It already feels too good and too familiar being wrapped up tight against him. Now he's taking me to hang out with his friends. People who are important to him.

Hang on heart, this ride's about to get bumpy.

CHAPTER TWENTY-ONE

Rooster

NOTHING WILL TOP TONIGHT FOR A LONG TIME.

Got to indulge in my favorite activities—fighting, fucking, and riding.

Most importantly, I got my girl on the back of my bike.

The night air has cooled off, but it's still humid as hell.

Finally, I make the turn for the long, dirt driveway that leads to the ranch. Iron gates mark the entrance to the property and two prospects from the Savage Dragons MC sweep their gazes over us before allowing us into the compound.

While the main building is still a good distance away, people are everywhere. Drunk and stumbling around. I take it slow up the road. Lights twinkle in the distance, people doing hell knows what out in the woods.

The parking area comes into view. I back the bike into one of the spots reserved for our club and shut it down.

Murphy and Heidi wave to us from their spot by the fire. They headed straight back here after leaving the Tipsy Saddle.

"Oh! Heidi has a leather vest like yours. I didn't know that," Shelby says. "Is she a member of your club, too?"

Before I have a chance to explain, Heidi turns to talk to one of the other girls. Next to me, Shelby stops moving. "Property of Murphy? What the—"

"It's club tradition," I cut her off, before she says something that will sour this whole night. "An honor. Means as much, if not more, than that diamond on her finger. Heidi's proud to wear her patch, and it lets everyone here know who she belongs to."

She seems to take a second to digest my words. "I guess when you put it that way, it's kind of romantic."

I let out a relieved breath. Last thing I need is her saying something insulting to one of the old ladies tonight. I like Shelby a hell of a lot, but I'd do almost anything to protect my brothers' women.

In the back of my mind, I note that the property patch doesn't freak her out.

Shelby fidgets, taking my attention off thoughts I have no business considering. She glances down at her outfit. "Am I okay here?"

It's a valid question. A quick look past the fire where a group of my brothers are gathered shows a lot of adult activity going on. Shit, half the yard is practically an orgy pit. "You're with me, Sugar." I sling my arm over her shoulders and steer her toward the fire.

"Are we going to your room? Or...?"

Did she assume I only brought her here to fuck? Or is she worried I want to join the porn-gone-wild crowd? Never happening. Hot rage sizzles though me at the thought of anyone else touching her. Even a brother. Fuck no. "You mind hanging out for a bit?"

"No, not at all."

I lean down and kiss her neck, tease her earlobe with my tongue. "Sugar, don't you worry. I'm plannin' to show you my room and ride you hard until the sun comes up."

"That right?" Her question's teasing, but she seems to relax.

"Fuck yeah. First, I want to introduce you to a few of my brothers."

"More than the ones I already met?"

"Whoever's not down here now, you'll meet tomorrow."

That seems to melt her remaining concerns away. She takes my hand. "Okay."

I laugh when I see who's joined the crowd tonight. "What dragged you out here, Wrath?" Upstate's enforcer is known for his brutal honesty and fighting skills, not socializing.

He points his bottle of beer at Murphy. "He did."

The beautiful blonde tucked close to Wrath's side

laughs. "Heidi said you were bringing Shelby Morgan back with you, and I had to say hello and tell her how awesome she is."

"Oh my goodness," Shelby mutters behind me.

Proud? Impressed? Hell, I'm not sure what I'm feeling, I pull Shelby forward and introduce her to Trinity. Heidi joins them, and they pepper Shelby with questions about music and the reality show.

She seems comfortable with Heidi and Trinity, so I shrug and snag a spot on the blanket next to Murphy. "Teller come down with you guys?"

"Nah, he's watching Alexa for us. Watching Grace, too." He glances around. "Rock and Hope were down here, but they disappeared into the woods a couple minutes ago."

That doesn't exactly surprise me. Although, I highly doubt those two are involved in any group fucking. More like a private party for two, and Rock will gut anyone who comes within fifty feet of his wife.

I'm looking forward to disappearing with Shelby soon and having our own private party.

Except, I kind of like her hanging out with the old ladies from my club. Seems like she spends so much time working, she doesn't have time for fun in her life.

Eventually, I pull her into my lap, and she rests her head on my shoulder.

I brush her hair off her face and run my fingers through it. "Tired?"

"Little bit."

"Had a long day."

She picks up her head and gives me a sexy smile. "And not much sleep."

Although I'd gotten distracted at her house, I've still got all sorts of questions for her. "So, do you play there every week?"

"I used to. A producer from *Roadhouse* saw me and asked me to audition for the show."

"Now I know why those cops treated you like a celebrity."

Her eyes widen. "Celebrity my ass! They gave me a ticket same as you."

I laugh at the memory. "First ticket I don't mind."

"Why's that?"

I kiss the tip of her nose. "Because I met you."

"That's—"

"Don't say it."

"Sweet."

I groan and squeeze her tighter.

Murphy stands and pulls Heidi up with him. "We're heading inside." He nudges Heidi.

Heidi's nervous gaze darts between Shelby and me. "Murphy's taking me boot shopping tomorrow. You're welcome to come. Or, if not, maybe you can recommend a place?"

"Yeah, I'd love to." Shelby seems really excited, but

then her shoulders drop and she turns to me. "I don't know what you..."

"That sounds good."

"We'll talk at breakfast." Murphy lift his chin at me. "Maybe we can find you a nice cowboy hat, too."

"I know a place." Shelby winks at me.

I flip Murphy off, and he returns the gesture before wrapping his arm around Heidi and leading her away.

Wrath and Trinity are the next to leave us.

"It was so great meeting you, Shelby." Trin leans in for a hug, and from what I've seen, Trin's not much of a hugger. "You definitely should've kicked Ruby's ass. So glad you got that tour. You're amazing."

I must have missed that part of their conversation, but Shelby seems pleased by the praise. "Thank you."

After they're gone, Shelby looks down at her hands like she's nervous or embarrassed or something.

"What's wrong?"

"Nothing. That was...surreal but so cool. Everyone around here knew I was on the show, but I never met anyone not from around here who...I mean I know people watched it all over but..."

"You know New York isn't located in Oz, right?"

She laughs softly and slaps my chest. "I know that."

"So, tell me, how long you been singing?"

She tips her head back and stares at the stars for a few minutes. Texas hill country nights have been gorgeous. As the heat fades with the sunset, the scent of wildflowers clings to the cooler air. Perfect night for stargazing, but all I can look at is Shelby.

"Long as I can remember," she finally answers. "Music's easier than talking sometimes."

"Your voice is beautiful. You were stunning on stage."

She blushes and ducks her head. "You don't even like country music."

"I like *your* music."

This time I get a smile. She turns and shifts in my lap. "Thank you for saying that."

"Sugar, one thing you should know about me, I don't say shit I don't mean."

"I see that about you, Logan." She moves again, straddling my lap, knees hugging my hips.

"Like it when you say my name."

She leans in and kisses my cheek and then moves over to my ear and sinks her teeth into my earlobe, sending zaps of electricity down my spine. "Thank you for coming to see me tonight. I was shocked you remembered."

"Couldn't figure out why you didn't want me to know where you worked. For a minute, I thought you might be a stripper."

"Trust me, more than one person's suggested that would be a more appropriate career for me."

Who the fuck said that to her? I'll rip their arms off. "Fuck that. You owned that stage. You transformed that shitty little bar into something else with your voice."

"You're exaggerating but thank you."

I press my palms against her cheeks, so she'll meet my eyes and understand every word is the truth. "I mean every single word, Sugar. Never thought anyone would get me to willingly listen to country music."

She tosses her head back and laughs, exposing the sexy column of her throat.

I run my hands up and down her legs and lean in to kiss her neck. "Really wish I hadn't let you change out of that dress."

Her hot breath skims over my cheek. "What would you do right now?"

Keeping my hands on her ass, I sit forward, pressing her against my erection. "I'd stroke that pretty little clit of yours until you were wet and begging for my cock again. Told you I didn't get enough before."

"You're insatiable."

Her eyes sparkle with desire, but I'm not done talking to her yet. I groan and can't believe I'm going to steer this conversation away from getting my dick inside her. "Tell me about this show you were on." I gesture toward the house. "Unlike the girls, I've never heard of it. What happened? How'd you end up on it?"

She tilts her head as if she's surprised I care more about information than fucking. Can't blame her, I'm surprised myself.

"Well, I didn't *win,* but I made it far enough for a jump start."

"Like?"

"I have a few singles up for digital download now."

"So, I can go buy a Shelby Morgan song anywhere I want?"

"Yes," she answers, with a proud chin lift. "But don't do that. I can send you whatever you want."

"Hell, no. I want to support my favorite artist. Gonna buy multiple copies everywhere I can."

"Now I'm your favorite, huh?"

"Damn right. What else?"

"About the show?" She scrunches up her nose and shifts her gaze over my shoulder. "Well, besides being betrayed by someone I thought was a friend, almost developing an eating disorder, and living under a microscope for eight weeks, it wasn't so bad."

That was a lot to take in, so I set aside my urge to go on a murder spree and wait to see if she wants to share more.

"Sorry." She glances down. "I don't mean to sound ungrateful."

"You can be honest with me, Shelby." Club life is all about staying under the radar, so I can't imagine the level of scrutiny she described. Sounds like absolute hell.

"It was a shock but also good for me to see the other side of the industry." Her face brightens. "And I landed an opening spot on a tour with Dawson Roads. It's a huge opportunity I never would've had otherwise."

"Now, *that* name I recognize."

She laughs and loops her arms around my neck. "Why doesn't that surprise me?"

"When's that happening?"

"In a couple weeks. That's why I'm doing rehearsals every morning. Playing when I can. Working extra shifts so I don't leave my mom high and dry." She bites her bottom lip. "There are a few dates of the tour in New York."

Damn, why does my heart pound even faster when she says that? I pull her closer and brush my lips against hers. "That so?"

She nods slowly.

"Think I can still get tickets?"

Her eyes widen. "You'd want to?"

"Fuck yeah. Why are you so surprised?"

She shrugs and looks away. "I'm not dumb, Rooster. A couple months from now, you probably won't remember my name."

I move my hand to the back of her head and pull her close. "You have no idea how wrong you are. I'll never forget you, Shelby."

"I won't forget you either. You've come to my rescue twice now."

"Happy to do it." I rub my thumb over her cheek. "I'm gonna need front row tickets and a backstage pass."

She nods slowly and stares into my eyes. "You'll always have an all-access pass, Logan."

I groan against her throat. "I'll hold you to that." I kiss her cheek and press my forehead against hers. "Are you up for boot shopping tomorrow?"

"Sure. I don't mind showing Heidi around." She hesitates. "If that's what you want to do."

"I want to see if we can find you a pair of *electric teal* boots."

She jiggles with laughter for a second then stops. "You don't have to buy me anything."

"I want to." I thrust my hips up, grinding what's rapidly becoming a painful erection against her. "Getting hard just thinking about you wearing them and nothing else."

"Never would've figured you for a boot fetish kinda guy."

"I'm surprised as anyone." Our teasing dies down, and somehow, I can't stop myself from opening my mouth and letting some truly sappy words pour out. "I want to get you something nice. So when you're out on the road, you'll wear them and remember how much of an awesome singer you are to make me love country music."

She doesn't laugh like I expected.

"Please don't." She covers my mouth with her fingers. "Don't make me like you any more than I already do."

Like. She has a point. Every time I'm with her, some other *L-word* keeps creeping into my mind. Something I've always told myself I'm not interested in. At all.

"Yeah," I whisper. "I like you a hell of a lot more than I ever expected, Shelby."

"Please." Her bottom lip quivers. "Don't do that. I can't afford a broken heart right now."

Hell no, I want to murder anyone who hurts her. I swallow hard. "The last thing I want to do is break your heart."

She grasps my cut, digging her fingers into the leather to pull me closer. Our lips crash together. Fire surges in my veins. My arms go around her, lifting her up. She hugs her knees to my hips and keeps on kissing me.

Never had anything in my life as perfect as her kisses.

Emotions I'm not familiar with roar inside me. What I said was true. I don't want to break her heart. But she might just be the first woman in a long time who's had the power to break mine.

AUTHOR NOTES

If you're new to the Lost Kings MC, welcome to the family! I hope you'll stick around and get to know the rest of the guys. If you're already part of the LOKI family, thank you so much for your support.

A shorter version of *Swagger and Sass* was included in the anthology, *Love, Loyalty, and Mayhem* that was only available from July to September 2019. After the success of *Love, Loyalty, and Mayhem*, I was really pleased with Rooster and Shelby's first story. I loved getting to know Rooster a bit better and I've been dying to write a country singer for a while now.

When I decided to re-release *Swagger and Sass* on its own, I wasn't supposed to expand it. *White Lies* was supposed to be my last release for 2019. But I had so many people who wrote and told me they'd missed *Love, Loyalty, and Mayhem* when it was available, that I knew I'd have to re-publish it sooner than I planned. So here it is!

Maybe it's a strange quirk unique to me, but I hate re-releasing things without any new content. It feels weird for some reason. And to be honest, even though I'd gone way over my word count for the *Love, Loyalty, and Mayhem* anthology, I had a few more scenes I'd wanted to write for *Swagger and Sass* that wouldn't necessarily fit into *Rhythm of the Road*. Re-releasing SAS gave me the perfect opportunity to add in those little bits!

I truly hope you appreciate the extra 7,000 or so words. And, well, if you didn't, feel free *not* to share that with me. It's okay.

My outlaw-motorcycle-club-meets-mafia-family-meets-rockstar-romance, *Kickstart My Heart*, is coming soon. You can read some (unedited, subject to change) episodes from it here for free if you'd like to get to know Chaser and Mallory before their first book is released!

Rhythm of the Road, Rooster and Shelby's first full-length story is available for pre-order now.

If you loved Rooster and Shelby's story, it would really mean a lot to me if you could leave a review at your favorite retailer. It does not have to be a long review. A few quick words about why you loved the book are more than enough. Leaving reviews is the *absolute best* way you can help your favorite authors (not just me!)

Thank you!

xo

Autumn

December 8, 2019

ABOUT THE AUTHOR

Autumn Jones Lake is the *USA Today* and *Wall Street Journal* bestselling author of over twenty novels, including the popular Lost Kings MC series. She believes true love stories never end.

Her past lives include baking cookies, bagging groceries, selling cheap shoes, and practicing law. Playing with her imaginary friends all day is by far her favorite job yet!

Autumn lives in upstate New York with her own alpha hero.

www.autumnjoneslake.com

facebook.com/autumnjoneslake

goodreads.com/autumnjoneslake

pinterest.com/autumnjoneslake

LOST KINGS MC

AN MC ROMANCE SERIES BY AUTUMN JONES LAKE

Printed in Great Britain
by Amazon

87879293R00092